Realm of
Unknowing

Other Books by Mark Rudman

POETRY:

By Contraries
The Nowhere Steps
Rider

CHAPBOOKS:

In the Neighboring Cell
The Mystery in the Garden
The Ruin Revived

PROSE:

Robert Lowell: An Introduction to the Poetry
Diverse Voices: Essays on Poets and Poetry

TRANSLATION:

My Sister—Life and The Highest Sickness, poems by Boris Pasternak
  (with Bohdan Boychuk)
Square of Angels: The Selected Poems of Bohdan Antonych
  (with Bohdan Boychuk)
Memories of Love: The Selected Poems of Bohdan Boychuk
Euripides' Daughters of Troy

Realm of
Unknowing

Meditations on Art, Suicide,
and Other Transformations

Mark Rudman

Wesleyan University Press

Published by University Press of New England
Hanover and London

Wesleyan University Press
Published by
University Press of New England
Hanover, NH 03755
© 1995 by Mark Rudman
Printed in the United States of America
5 4 3 2 1
CIP data appear at the end of the book

Grateful acknowledgment is made to the editors of the following periodicals in which versions of these essays appeared:

Arion, "William Arrowsmith in Heaven"; *Columbia Magazine*, "Father's Wild Game"; *Denver Quarterly*, " 'A Non-Figurative, Perceptual Realist With Existential Overtones': On Jake Berthot"; *Pequod*, "Catastrophe Practice: On Nicholas Mosley"; *Raritan*, "The Night: On Michelangelo Antonioni"; *Southwest Review*, "On Place: City and Country" (sections of which also appeared in *American Letters and Commentary*, under the title "Change of Season"); *Tikkun*, "My Best Friend."

The poem "Dreams of Cities" first appeared in *Boulevard*; "The Art of Dying" in *Raritan*; and "Oscillation: San Francisco" (section 2) in *Threepenny Review*.

"William Arrowsmith in Heaven" was selected as one of the Notable Essays of the Year by *Best American Essays 1994*.

Excerpt from "Bare Almond-Trees" by D. H. Lawrence, from *The Complete Poems of D. H. Lawrence* by D. H. Lawrence, edited by V. de Sola Pinto and F. W. Roberts. Copyright © 1964, 1971 by Angelo Ravagli and C. M. Weekly, Executors of the Estate of Frieda Lawrence Ravagli. Used by permission of Viking Penguin, a division of Penguin Books USA Inc.

Selections from William Arrowsmith's translations of Eugenio Montale, *Cuttlefish Bones* (© 1992), *The Occasions* (© 1987), and *The Storm and Other Things* (© 1985), are reprinted by permission of W. W. Norton & Co.

Excerpt from George Oppen, *Collected Poems*, © 1968 by George Oppen, reprinted by permission of New Directions.

To Madelaine, Sam, and Marjorie

The Art of Dying

To the Suicides of '50 and '54
(Cesare Pavese, Herbert Leeds)

Even to say something went wrong is wrong:
you merely took control of your own death;
and what could be more futile than trying

to pin it down on some one thing, some
reason, a woman lost, some form
of failure, imagination dead.

You had had enough of the same
and somehow that absence grew
large enough to swallow you.

Not the woman with the hoarse voice.
Not the mayhem and slaughter
on the bridge at Remagen.

Not the hills leveled.
Not the rows of hazel cut down.
The rye fields gone.

1972. The Seine. A bleached
summer afternoon. Paul Celan
jumped in and Jean Vigo did not do

himself in exactly but hurried
his tubercilli by shooting
L'Atalante *on a barge in the hard*

November rain. It must be
an absence at the heart, a hole that grows
until it swallows you up

until you are no more: it's then,
when you're already done in,
that you do yourself in:

every breakdown is a catastrophe
that has already occurred—
a burst of anger

is never sudden, the thing
most feared in secret
always happens.

CONTENTS

PREFACE

We write because we sense that something remains to be done, because no one else, to our amazement, has addressed the questions that torment us from an angle we find satisfactory. Such as suicide. Such as ecstasy. Why, with regard to the problem of other minds, is philosophy so anxious to discount the possibility that there can be an absolute conception of reality that is not peculiar to any point of view?

In an era of specialization, we are forced into the realm of partial knowledge, technical expertise, and lose track of the whole. Information multiplies and wisdom dwindles. Art and philosophy push aside the larger questions.

Each essay in *Realm of Unknowing* is a "raid on the inarticulate," a series of forays—sparked by a certain disturbance: the mention of my obscure uncle, Herbert I. Leeds, in the *New Yorker*, which provoked me to explore the black hole his death created in what was once a close-knit, colorful and supportive family; an Antonioni retrospective that occurred at a time when the interest in his films was dangerously close to nil; a weekly commute to Purchase during the Gulf War; a newspaper item (many years ago) reporting that my childhood schoolmate in Chicago had killed his grandmother because she wouldn't buy him a pair of chino pants, which gave rise to "My Best Friend," a memoir as much concerned with intimacy and eros, as experienced by prepubescent children, as with class and race.

I proceed dialectically; the searches are based on opposition: city/country, "failure"/"success," poverty/wealth, intimacy/distance. The mosaic form that they take on mirrors what the essays struggle to convey; the sentence, paragraph or section as a unit—parallel perhaps to the stanza in a poem or the triadic structure of a sonnet—allows me to touch only on what compels me, on what is necessary, and to explore how the margin informs the center without having to, in the Balzacian sense, spend pages describing the furniture in the room.

Failure, ruin, suicide; this dark hydra-headed trio shadows our lives in different ways. But I use these terms suggestively. For example, Antonioni and the painter Jake Berthot embrace an existential notion of danger, while the classicist William Arrowsmith skirts failure (while living under the threat of its cloud breaking open on him) by not subjecting his own "finished work" to public scrutiny.

Whether the subjects be famous, obscure, artistic, streetwise, or somewhere in between, it is the process of inquiry that compels me. The difficulties that the artist-figures encounter parallel and illuminate the human tragedy that explodes in the more explicitly autobiographical essays. Just as the essay on my uncle, "Realm Beyond Knowing," and "Father's Wild Game" (based on a title of one of his films) are in close dialogue with and in some ways clarify each other, the essays on Antonioni, Arrowsmith, Berthot, and the characters in "My Best Friend" form another group. The theme of place takes many forms throughout the book, which ends with an interrogation of what "place" is and—perhaps more important from a metaphysical perspective—*is not* in "On Place: City and Country."

I see the essays as mirroring each other at oblique angles, as organically connected, almost as if spores floated between them, augmenting the diverse themes, making them into a book.

I would like to thank Charles Ardia, William Everson, Francis Nevins, Gilberto Perez, Kryssa Schemmerling, and Charles Silver and The Museum of Modern Art for their help with the essays on film. I am also grateful to Megan Abbott, Richard Locke, Charlie Smith, and Katharine Washburn for their encouragement, dialogue, and commentary.

South Londonderry, Vermont, 1994

Realm Beyond Knowing

Something cracks in your life. You are finished. The world cracks.

—Nicholas Mosley

I

I always like to read what's playing at the revival houses even when I'm out of town. That's how I noticed that *The Man Who Wouldn't Die*, directed by Herbert I. Leeds, my mother's brother, was playing at Theater 80 St. Marks. I had never seen any of his films. I tore out the notice. When I got back to the city, I called the theater. The man at St. Marks had seen this and one other film by Herbert I. Leeds from the Mike Shayne series, but *The Man* was the best.

2

The director of *The Man Who Wouldn't Die* died by his own hand in the spring of 1954. He was forty-four years old.

3

When I pass the apartment where I lived as a child, I also pass the Blackstone Hotel, a name whose dark syllables are forever branded on my brain because that is where he shot himself in the chest on May 15th, his step-mother's birthday.

In my one strong memory of him we are waiting for a table at a restaurant called Tappan Hill, in a place just north of the city called Tappan Hill. We are sprawled on an immense lawn which sloped down toward a pond. My uncle, in his bulky tweed sportscoat (why was he dressed so warmly on a warm afternoon?), is showing me how to identify a four-leaf clover.

We never found one, but he discounted many of the three-leaved ones I plucked with sublime, magisterial patience and tranquillity (qualities my grandfather and mother never displayed). "I've got one!" I'd shout and place it in his palm. He'd squint and peel back the petals and say "Look— one . . . two . . . three—that's all." *You have to look long and long at things if you want to see what they really are,* he was urging me; *the point is to be clear and not hide behind imposture. There is an economy in nature. Anyone can try to push a three-leaf clover as a four, but it is better to own up to what you've got and what you haven't got. Why embellish, when you can go on looking . . . ?* He made me want to search, and not be satisfied with approximations, or things that others might take for the truth because they weren't interested enough in these details. I could sense he was memorizing my movements, that this was the first time he had ever really paid willing attention to me. (He had a daughter, just a year younger than myself, in a family obsessed with boys. My grandfather, whose nickname was "Tarzan," called me—and my uncle—"boy.") The gnats and flies, bees and wasps, danced around our heads. He didn't swat them away. He liked insects! It must have been the fall before he died. I had just turned five the previous winter. If it had been a year earlier, I doubt I would remember the scene so vividly.

4

Herbert I. Leeds (Levy) was a film director—almost exclusively of B's and sequels. All the witnesses agree that he had a reputation as a difficult man. I remember well the story of his fight with the screenwriter Samuel G. Engel. The script called for the Cisco Kid to "pull a guitar out of his saddlebags." My uncle refused to "shoot" this "impossibility," and the screenwriter showered him with threats. When my grandfather told me the story, he emphasized my uncle's intelligence, and when my mother told me the story, she emphasized his arrogance.

One night I dreamt my uncle was alive, sitting at a blue iron table at pool's edge, planning a new script. I want to ask him questions about his life, but his concentration on the script is total. He throws me a look of disdain, grabs my camera, puts his hand over the lens and says, "I'll talk, but first you have to turn that off. *I* stand on that side of the camera."

5

My uncle not only directed mysteries, he was a mystery. My grandfather talked about him all the time until his face, already hard to read behind his blind man's dark glasses, became drained of all expression and his voice broke. My mother answered my questions about him with a high degree of irritation because (a) he's dead; (b) she hardly knew him; (c) he never smiled; (d) he was bossy, imperious, an off-the-set director. "I just don't know, I just don't know why you want to dig around the mounds of the dead."

Her problems with the significant men in her life make these questions all the more painful for her to consider, and I can't seem to get her to register that I was infinitely closer, physically in early childhood and later spiritually, to her father than my own, and he spoke to me often of his son.

.   .   .

"But his life was—tragic."

"That's right."

"Aristotle says the first requirement for tragedy is a fall from a high place . . ."

"Your father did that. Not Bert. He did himself in in a squalid hotel room. He did himself in good all right. And I was there to pick up the pieces. And gather up the needles. Discreetly."

"Heroin?"

"Probably morphine."

"Any idea why?"

"I guess he thought he had no future. Things weren't great between him and Evelyn. He couldn't find work after the war and had to live on handouts from his father."

"Evelyn was so pretty."

"She had a pretty face. But she had piano legs."

I wish my mother hadn't said that. Prior to hearing "piano legs" I had seen Evelyn as a beautiful and decorous woman, not as a creature maimed by imperfect—legs. Why should the size of her legs be so important? Even as a child, it disturbed me to break women up into component parts.

Now when my aunt sat across from me on her impeccable beige sofa, it was as if her calves had detached themselves from her knees and sat there quietly, stolidly, with the rest of her body, which, come to think of it, was strangely immobile. When she crossed her legs or rose to fix someone a drink, the piano legs remained beside the sofa—in their high-heeled shoes. They had eyes and a mouth, like dolls.

Still, I felt flattered when she smiled at me, when she, who was "above" so many things, descended to my level with a smile. I was either too young or too dense to pick up the condescension. I thought she genuinely liked me and thought my wild enthusiasms and tale-telling were "cute." I would embroider an anecdote and I'd watch her lips part, slightly, slowly, almost breaking into a smile. . . . I was shrewd enough to sense that she was indulging me and fueling my exaggerations, but not that she was patronizing me and wishing all the time that I was not there—not wishing me dead, merely gone.

She was a brittle woman—absolutely wrong for my uncle even on a good day. I can imagine him becoming apoplectic while she sat there looking superior. I am not saying she was cruel but that she had a misguided sense of her own superiority because she came from a well-known mercantile family and because, looking at her own face in the mirror, probably wondered how such a fate could have befallen a well-bred beauty such as herself.

After all, she'd been divorced from my uncle, and it didn't exactly thrill her to see his family. It was a chore.

. . .

Our conversations about Herbert Leeds always came back to a central core of "facts": he was sent to preparatory schools in Switzerland, where he "got his French." Accepted at Yale and Lehigh, he chose Lehigh to be near his cousin Arnold, who (later to become an actor's agent) liked to "live high." He came to love the West and could not get used to New York after being surrounded by so much space.

. . .

And so I thought: Why not try and see some of his films and track down a few of the people who knew him, and see where that leads?

Given that all I could think about while in school was being out of school, and my aversion to the smell of libraries and the delirious dust of stacks, I proceeded cautiously. The peremptory information listed in *Halliwell's Film Directory* was no help in beginning to track down Bert's films.

I called "detective" Charles Ardai, an ex-student of mine who, even as an undergraduate, was already an accomplished writer of mystery stories and editor of mystery magazines and anthologies. He contacted Mike Nevins, a mystery writer, film historian, and professor of law at the University of Missouri, who wrote me a letter listing Herbert Leeds's films and highlighting screenwriters such as Borden Chase, actors such as Claire Trevor, and cinematographers such as Arnand D'Usseau who worked with him.

. . .

Why didn't Bert try to direct for television if he merely wanted to buy time? According to Mike Nevins, he did, and made a *Life of Riley* episode with Jackie Gleason in the title role and several "Cisco"s, including "Bullets and the Booby Trap" with "Bobby" Blake, who though known to me from *In Cold Blood* and *Beretta*, had been an actor all of his life and had undergone many deaths and rebirths.

I know very little about Robert Blake, but among the little I know is that he had a drug problem and talked openly about his cure—about, I should add, the difficulty of his cure, for Blake is nothing if not rough around the edges.

He also starred in *Tell 'Em Willie Boy Is Here* (1970), the first film that Abraham Polonsky had made since *Force of Evil* in 1948. Polonsky, a Marxist, made several classics in the '40s before he was blacklisted.

"Polonsky," Andrew Sarris writes in *The American Cinema*, "along with Chaplin and Losey, remains one of the casualties of the anti-communist hysteria of the fifties."

My uncle wasn't blacklisted. Both he and my grandfather were hysterical anti-Communists.

In *In Cold Blood* and *Tell 'Em Willie Boy Is Here*, Blake plays an outcast. In *Willie Boy* he plays an Indian who, having committed murder in self-defense, is hunted down reluctantly by sheriff Robert Redford, and if I remember correctly, he asks Redford to shoot him when he's cornered in the blinding sun among the red rocks of the canyon rather than face incarceration—rather, the humiliation of incarceration by the gloating righteous white men lusting for his death in the brutal, barbaric town.

Having cut class to catch the noon performance of *Willie Boy* the day it opened in New York, I remember the silence between the ricochet of every gunshot of that sequence, two men alone in the open, coming to terms.

.   .   .

But I'm getting ahead of myself. This search began not when I read that *The Man Who Wouldn't Die* was playing at Theater 80 St. Marks but when my friend Rachel Hadas, after reading a review of Elia Kazan's autobiography in the *Threepenny Review*, called to tell me how much Kazan reminded her of my father. I was thinking that myself—reading the review at the moment that she called—and got hold of the book right away. But my first thought on obtaining it was to look up my uncle's name in the index and scan the page where Kazan "*ordered* Herbert Leeds, our secretary, to call a meeting of the Directors Guild" (my emphasis).

My uncle, in my mother's account, liked to do the ordering. Even during his last days he had the newspaper delivered to his room at the Blackstone, needing to tip the bellboy a buck, rather than go downstairs and get it for a nickel at the newsstand.

6

The "Blake" connection doesn't pan out: I'm new at this game of tracking down celebrities, but I take Charles Ardai's advice and call ICM (International Creative Management) in L.A. No sooner have I dialed the number than someone—whose voice sounds like a machine—answers the phone and gives me the number of Robert Blake's agent. But the punkish twang, the child's voice caught in a man's throat, on the other end of the line is unmistakably Blake's. "Yeah. Who's this. Whaddya want." "I'm trying to find out some infor—" "You got the wrong guy. I'm no longer in the business." "Wait. I'm trying to find out some information about Herbert Leeds." "Look. I told you. You got the wrong guy. I'm not in the business anymore." "But—" "Call me tomorrow." He hangs up. I call him tomorrow. "Who?" "Were you in *Bullets and the Booby Trap* in the early fifties, a—" I am about to say, "Cisco Kid segment." "You got the wrong guy. I told you. I'm not in the business anymore." He hangs up.

I said he was rough around the edges—but this is more like sandpaper. But what could Blake, then "Bobby" Blake, who would have been no more than ten or so at the time, have been able to tell me to throw any light on what my uncle's aspirations were or to what extent his suicide resulted from the frustration of his talent and intelligence within a studio system where he was consigned to B movies for most of his career?

7

My father's suicide—and the steps leading up to it—has led me to think harder than I might have about people who are on the brink of ruin. Because there are other possibilities in the end, before the end, than ruin. There are people who are staggered by every defeat, every battle lost, and people who always "pop up" (as my son would say) like a jack-in-the-box, ready to try something else. When hearing of someone's ruin, especially someone who once enjoyed a privileged circumstance, I often fantasize what else they might have done instead of taking their own life in what would prove to be their final crisis.

.   .   .

I arrive at a picnic at my son's school: one of his classmates (already bespectacled at the tender age of six), stands, soaking, next to a puddle, his mouth open wide: the indignation is too much. And my son leans down, puts his hands on his knees, and inspects the puddle, as if waiting for it to leap up again. He is looking into it like a window. Like a spiral, it has no proper beginning or end.

Children, when they experience something that delights them (from a card trick to the merry-go-round), will ask to "do it again."

This is what the suicide relinquishes: the chance to see the morning light caress a leaf one more time. . . .

8

I have only been able to track down two of my uncle's films in New York, *Mr. Moto in Danger Island* and *Island in the Sky*.

Watching *Mr. Moto in Danger Island* at the Museum of Modern Art (the only film they have by Leeds in their archive), I had the sense of efficiency and clarity, of precision in the swift progression from scene to scene.

I felt quite spoiled watching this 35mm print alone with my wife on plush leather seats in the immense art-theater-size screening room with the private projectionist yawning away in his booth.

"Nothing is too good for Mr. Moto," said Charles Silver, the genial curator of MOMA's film archive.

The Mr. Moto series was already well tried by the time my uncle was assigned as director. And Peter Lorre's characterization of the famous detective was already well established: his ability to shrink his body and wrinkle his forehead to convey thoughts; Lorre's subtle facial and eye movements that belie the banality of the dialogue and his predictable revelations: ratiocination in the lower case.

The film opens with a wrestling scene on a ship, and for a moment I thought we were in my uncle's territory: athletics (Ward Bond played one of the wrestlers). The next—and last—thing to strike me was that the men were all tiny—the very opposite of my tall, broad-shouldered uncle and his father. There was something ludicrous, in particular, about the diminutive colonel with all his stripes and squeaky voice. Did my uncle cast against type intentionally? Or did he scale the other actors down to not dwarf the diminutive Lorre?

I tried to imagine how Bert put the boat chase together in the cutting room, from shots of the cast on one boat to the diamond smuggler speeding away in another: when the latter had his back to the camera, it looked like stock footage.

Everything I can uncover about my uncle is a slight clue. But unlike Mr. Moto, who, when he goes to a library on the island (which is not some reef or jut of sand but the "real" Puerto Rico) and asks to see *the last books the dead man had taken out*, is led to the marsh where he finds a trace of the special mud that will lead him to the villain, I am led only to further speculations around an empty center.

9

My uncle learned his trade in the cutting room and probably never did anything better than his second film, *Island in the Sky* (1938).

The city swirls against the darkness of the morning and the heat around the vertical sign of the Wellington Hotel. I am crossing Sixth Avenue at 10:00 A.M. on a Monday morning in June on my way to MOMA, with *Island in the Sky*, on loan from film historian William Everson, under my arm in its metal case, the past and future raveling and unraveling, with the sense that the city is neither indifferent nor caring, but here I am, thirty-five years after my uncle's death, digging up his films, in search of something.

The plot: A bad guy, Peter Doyle, who seems to be the link tying together the disparate threads of the mystery, is doing time in Blackgate Prison. The dead man, thought to have been killed by his son, is not the young man's real son but Doyle's ex-teacher, whom Doyle employed to act the role of the boy's father to give him a good foundation in life: a bizarre twist on paternity.

The hero (played by Michael Whalen), an Assistant D.A., looks so competent we trust he can handle his work with "one hand tied behind his back." The heroine (played by Gloria Stuart) is his secretary, soon to be his wife.

She's lithe, alert, and alive. He is handsome and quick-witted. But when the phone is brought to their table, at the nightclub run by the gangsters, with the inevitable call—"we got a dead man here on Eleventh Street"— he's annoyed that their dinner has been interrupted. The very gangsters he consorts with are the ones whose plot to cheat Jimmy Doyle leads to the man's death. But he doesn't care—he's a high liver—on the seventy-second floor in the penthouse nightclub—Island in the Sky. All he can think about is handling the case with dispatch: getting the conviction that is obvious. He is unwilling to let any doubt enter his own consciousness and willing to overlook small clues. His secretary's curiosity about the case annoys him.

(Michael Whalen looks a lot like Robert Donat, and he and Gloria Stuart together look so much like Donat and Madeleine Carroll in *The Thirty-Nine Steps*, it makes me wonder if Bert didn't cast the couple with the earlier film in mind.)

Stuart first sees Doyle working in the library, an exemplary prisoner who is obsessed with saving his son. And it is only through Stuart's energy and drive that Doyle's son, wrongly accused of murdering his father (who as I have said was not his father anyway), is saved from an imminent death sentence.

In the final sequence of the film, Stuart and Whalen are trapped in a closet at the Island in the Sky nightclub when the shoot-out begins. The action is protracted, as if taking place in a dream, underwater, in an otherwise swiftly moving film. Throughout the sequence, they're banging wildly on the door, and when at last they get it open, Whalen finally perks up and dives toward the villain (Leon Ames) and tackles him—he flings himself like a man who has one shot at redemption: he knows, finally, what is to be done.

Michael Whalen makes the character of the D.A. appear to embody values that he doesn't have. His decency is deceptive. Without his secretary's intervention he would have let an innocent man die. He's not interested in the almost absurd intersection of various fates. All he does is warn Gloria Stuart not to get in too deep. (*Remember, the sooner this case is over, dear, the sooner we go on our honeymoon.*)

· · ·

In the scene where they discover the dead man I find an immediate parallel between the body slumped on the floor, killed by a shotgun blast, and the image of my uncle's body slumped on the floor of the Blackstone Hotel. This is one of the first sequences he ever shot.

Was he thinking of it when he pulled the trigger? (We know from his obituary in the *New York Herald* what he'd underlined in the book he was reading—"I'm so sorry to do what I'm doing. I'm so ashamed"—but not the name of the book.)

Already unsettled by the man's slumped body and the mention of Blackgate Prison, the prominent appearance of the stringently vertical sign for the Wellington Hotel, the most striking object in a night street sequence in the movie almost scares—and thrills—me. The angle and feeling of the street are identical to the way it is now, fifty years after the film was shot. The Wellington Hotel gives a frame to Manhattan even in the few glimpses we get of it out the rear window of the coupe.

.　.　.

The man, as Michael Whalen plays him, reminds me a good deal of my uncle, though more brittle and controlled. The character has addressed himself to function, to how things operate. Like a film cutter, or editor.

.　.　.

The Assistant D.A. is like a father who, to all appearances, does all the right things and yet is senseless to the deeper needs of his family and, ultimately, to his community. I don't mean "senseless" lightly. I mean incurious. His selfishness begins to seem monstrous the more his secretary/fiancée searches and he sits back at his desk to receive her reports, only to toss them aside. He can't involve himself in life beyond the sheer cliff of his desire to be away from this mess and with her—on an island somewhere.

The ex-gangster and the D.A.'s assistant are the heroes because they do change—and the film is hopeful in an unsentimental way about the possibilities of change. Like several B movies with Gloria Stuart (whom Bert found very difficult to direct) it is a vehemently feminist film.

. . .

I'm on my way out of the museum when I glimpse an earthwork by Robert Smithson: several mirrors on the floor topped with a chunk of coral. Your eyes strike the coral first but then are drawn to what you see in the mirror, your own feet, the ceiling, odds and ends of bodies passing, escalator rails. Smithson was not trying to get us just to look at the coral but at the world—the whole earth.

Smithson's *Spiral Jetty* constantly returns toward its point of origin, and it never touches base; rather, it continues onward and around. A spiral never closes. Each ending is a point of departure.

10

My uncle did not die in the Blackstone Hotel. He died in the Wyndham Hotel. And it is only too just that I should discover this fact on the morning I am preparing to leave Windham, Vermont, where I spent the summer in the hills. The news clippings sent to me in Windham at this unpropitious hour all attest to this fact. But I would wager, odds on, that the Wyndham did become the Blackstone and that my mother, in telling me he died in the Blackstone, was emphasizing that he died in the hotel across the street from where his father lived, no matter what the name.

It is painful to leave Windham, especially these last days that are the precursors of autumn: wind roaring in the black trees, which thrash like western heroes untying themselves after the bad guys have walked out the door; the fields bending and waving; the pitch-black sky lit with an unearthly blue at the horizon; the half moon over the still pond in the morning; the yellow of dandelions and goldenrod stark against the blue sky.

11

The intoxicating titles of Herbert Leeds's films constitute a kind of biography. Here's the list, along with my first reaction before I had seen any of them. *Love on a Budget* (appropriate for the twenty-six-year-old first-time director's elation); *Island in the Sky* (with its Baudelairean balconies of heaven); *Keep Smiling* (grim prospect); *Five of a Kind* (brings in the element of risk and danger—too much of a good thing is no good); *The Arizona Wildcat* (spirited young girl); *Mr. Moto in Danger Island* (work with Peter Lorre, good, good); *The Return of the Cisco Kid* (I don't like that "return"); *Chicken Wagon Family* (how could they do it to him?); *City in Darkness* (with Sidney Toler as Charlie Chan, good, good); *The Cisco Kid and the Lady* (chivalrous implications); *Yesterday's Heroes* (he was about to become one after the war); *Romance of the Rio Grande* (leaves me cold); *Ride On, Vaquero* (fabulous, spirited title); *Blue, White, and Perfect* (but you can't get blue in black and white); *The Man Who Wouldn't Die* (the irony of this needs no assist from me); *Just Off Broadway* (where my uncle stood in relation to A pictures); *Manila Calling* (beachy, tropical agit-prop— helmet on helmet, hill on hill); *Time to Kill* (not in a sixty-minute version of Raymond Chandler's *The High Window*); *It Shouldn't Happen to a Dog* (shouldn't have happened to him); then, as if in a prophetic coda to the circumstances of his aftermath: *Let's Live Again*; *Bunco Squad* (men get to be boys); *Father's Wild Game* (he endured it: his father "Tarzan"'s life was a "wild game" which he imagined he won).

12

While I have resigned myself to not seeing all of my uncle's films, I feel I do need to see certain ones to get a sense of the range of his talent and search for possible correspondences between scenes and images in his films and his life. It is devilishly hard to find anything, and I am on the brink of losing patience when I set up an appointment with Rosemary Hanes at the Library of Congress to screen *Bunco Squad* and *The Cisco Kid and the Lady* in Washington in September. She gives me the number of someone in the legal department of 20th Century–Fox, and my heart sinks at having to approach a bureaucracy.

"Who are you?"

"A writer."

"We usually grant permission only to people who are connected with a university."

"I am. NYU."

"I'm sure that NYU has a Fax. Could you put your request in writing?"

"I'm not at NYU now. I'm in Vermont."

"Then you can write us a letter."

"Sure."

"Then you're not in a wild rush."

"No."

"You must be very organized." (This is the first time in my life I've been accused of being "very organized.") "Most people who call want everything done right away."

I have already wasted this precious time calling 20th Century–Fox and putting a request in writing to see some of the films (which would probably mean spending at least a thousand dollars on planes and motels and rented cars) when Rosemary Hanes calls back, having consulted several catalogs and spoken to a friend who is an expert in these matters, to say she's tracked down *City in Darkness* and that it's available at Eddie Brandt's Saturday Matinee in Los Angeles.

I saw half a dozen Charlie Chan films, some with Sidney Toler, for rent at the Video Store in Manchester last week. I couldn't help wondering why, since they seemed to have almost the whole series, it had to be *City in Darkness* that was missing.

"Sure, we have *City in Darkness*, both for sale and for rent," says Donavan at Eddie Brandt's. "Anything else I can do for you?"

It's a peculiar twist of this project that only the films I'm least interested in, like this and other sequels, are easy to find.

"I'm looking for anything by Herbert Leeds."

"What are some of the names of the films?"

"*The Arizona Wildcat* . . ."

"I think we have that. Tell me his name again."

"Herbert Leeds."

He starts to rattle off the names of the films; he must have brought his name up on the computer.

"*Island in the Sky* . . . Now that's really hard to find."

"Really? I borrowed a print."

"You *saw Island in the Sky*?"

Now I'm going to hear that this film is well known to cultists? Why wouldn't Everson have told me that?

"It was good."

"I'll bet. It's with John Wayne, right?"

"John Wayne? No. This is with Gloria Stuart and Michael Whalen."

"Oh. Must be *The Island in the Sky*. But we have *Ride, Vaquero*." I can't believe my luck.

"Great!"

"With Robert Taylor, right?"

"No, Cesar Romero. And it's *Ride* On, *Vaquero*."

"Oh yeah, we have *Ride, Vaquero*. We don't rent it, we lend it free under the counter if you rent another film."

"Maybe I should see it anyway," given, I think, how I'm using some of these titles; my search for correspondences.

"No problem. We have *Bunco Squad* too, free."

"Send it."

"And *Manila Calling*."

"Send it."

"And a bunch of Mike Shayne films. But those are all rentals." Doesn't he understand that I need a few rentals to help pay for the freebees recorded off TNT?

"Have you seen any of the Shayne series?"

"All of them."

"How are they?"

"Great."

Great?

"A lot of that B movie stuff is great."

"True."

"But I have a confession to make."

"OK."

"I think that *City in Darkness* is the worst of the Charlie Chan films with Sidney Toler. But it's not your uncle's fault. It's a bad script."

. . .

"Hey, I think I can even find you a glossy photograph of your uncle on the set."

"Great."

"Hold on. We have posters too."

"Great."

"But if we're talking posters, we're talking real money."

"Not so great."

.   .   .

By the time this conversation ends I will await receiving seven of his movies, three "under the counter" (free) by mail within a week, and they will put *Time to Kill* and *The Man Who Wouldn't Die* on a cassette for $29.99. I hang up the phone with an elation that must be akin to that of an archaeologist finding a skeleton at a dig. . . .

.   .   .

For once my hunch is was right: *The Arizona Wildcat* was about an adolescent girl. Played by Jane Withers.

.   .   .

Every interviewer is prepared for the fact that most people prefer to talk about themselves rather than others. My conversation with Jane Withers is no exception. Still, it yielded several pearls. I reach her on August 26, 1991. She is on her way to see *Five of a Kind*, the other film she made with my uncle, for the first time in forty years. Some of her fans had unearthed it; she has no idea how, but she's sure there is no way I could procure it from them.

I try to calculate the odds of her going to view *Five of a Kind* on the very night I contact her about my uncle, and while I first think how impossibly long the odds would be, on reflection I reverse this opinion. The very fact that these fans have dug up *Five of a Kind* now after all these years is somehow consonant with my project; the fact that I have undertaken this search increases the possibility (like a sudden shift of particles on the molecular plane) that she should be going to see *Five of a Kind* tonight.

My uncle, how did she find him? The best, the most sensitive and intelligent man she ever met, ever worked with, the only one "who really directed" her, that is, told her what to do. ("I was a kid and they expected me to act!") He took the time to talk to her. He said, "Janey, you're one of a kind, you're unique." The others "just told [her] to act and [she] was just a kid, on the radio at two and in child roles in the movies after that. I was an adult before I was a kid." He was "loved by everybody that he worked with. The one word I'd choose to say what he was like is *kindness*." He had brown-velvet, chocolate eyes. He knew she loved dolls, and every year he sent her a doll. She has fourteen thousand dolls and ten thousand teddy bears and has collected the particularly precious dolls made by Linsey, one of the Dionne quints, who play themselves in *Five of a Kind*.

She always wondered what happened to my uncle and had no idea that he was dead, much less a suicide. She herself left Hollywood in the '40s, married and ran a ranch in Texas, where she cooked for fifteen cowboys. All she didn't do was brand cattle.

She was in very few movies after that. *Bright Eyes. Giant.*

I mention my uncle's dislike of Zanuck. "Oh, everyone hated that horrible man."

Does she have any idea why he came to such an untimely end?
    "Oh yes. He was much too kind and sensitive. He couldn't take the world he was living in."
    "Do you mean Hollywood in particular? I think he may have found the whole idea of Hollywood difficult after the war."
    "No, just the world."

Jane Withers offers this so assertively that I decide not to pursue this line of questioning any more.

· · ·

Who is Jane Withers? She was a child star. At the age of two, she claims, she had a radio show with "ten million listeners." Shirley Temple always played the good girl, and Jane Withers played the bad girl. She played it so well that she "upstaged Shirley Temple."

Her self-estimation is not far from what Brian Garfield says about her in the paragraph he devotes to *The Arizona Wildcat* in his study of Western films:

Carillo, a former bandit turned stagecoach driver, adopts a scrappy orphan. Amusing comedy has a lot of action, well suited to the genial adolescent girl star who nearly supplanted Shirley Temple in the hearts of Fox execs if not of the public.

13

I am most often wrong in my guesses. When I discovered that *Five of a Kind* was not about gambling but about quintuplets, I was discouraged. Looking through one of my few film books, *Graham Greene on Film*, my eye lights on the name Jean Hersholt, which I remember, not from its parenthetical position in my uncle's filmography but from my conversation with Jane Withers, who offered, amidst her free associations, how wonderful he was as the doctor. I learn that *Five of a Kind* was a sequel, perhaps not the first, to *The Country Doctor*, about which Greene, comparing it not unfavorably to Chekhov, wrote: "The theme is serious, the treatment has an unusual edge. . . ."

John Mosher, the *New Yorker*'s film critic, found little to redeem my uncle's sequel and wrote off *Five of a Kind*, "this . . . third of the Dionne series," by saying that while the quintuplets are barely "before the camera" for twenty minutes, the film owes whatever quality it has to their presence.

14

Only now, thinking about the chronology of Bert's films, does the significance of his death in May of 1954 come home to me. My mother had already remarried, in February of that year, and we had already moved from Manhattan to Chicago Heights, a town "where all the gangsters lived" on the outskirts of Chicago, where my mother had fled, whisking me off like some innocent on the run from the mob—to get me away from her father, who "imagined he was my father," before he could "do to me what he did to—Bert."

No wonder I don't remember any sorrowful dark aura in the aftermath of his death. I was already in Illinois and did not hear my grandfather bellowing and weeping—a broken king.

15

I call my old teacher at Columbia, Andrew Sarris, to see if he might have any tips on how I might begin, where I might look, who I might talk to. He has heard of Herbert I. Leeds, and though he can't remember seeing any of his films, he recognizes him as "one of those Poverty Row directors."

I mention that I am about to look up the reviews of the films in the *New York Times*. "You won't find anything there. Nobody took those films seriously then."

Sarris is right. On the morning I "screen" *Island in the Sky* I duck into MOMA's film library. The reviews are patronizing, as if the reviewers were tired of encountering yet another genre piece, much less a sequel: another mystery, another western. The reviews concentrate on incongruities in the plot and make no mention of the direction or camera work at all. It is as if directors of films like *The Man Who Wouldn't Die* never—in terms of film history—lived.

. . .

When that oddly dour screwball comedy *It Shouldn't Happen to a Dog* plays on American Movie Channel, the host highlights the Doberman's canny performance and says not one word about the man who got the dog to act.

. . .

The *Times* review of *Manila Calling*, his last film with Lloyd Nolan and Carole Landis (soon to kill herself in a fit of rage at Rex Harrison for dumping her) is dismissive.

"Sol Wurtzel (the producer) . . . has seized upon the idea of using the Japanese invasion of the Phillipines [*sic*] as the background for a story similar to that of [John Ford's] *The Lost Patrol*. . . ." The director—who is not named—"simply made use of clichés. . . ."

Sarris told me that the cult director Joseph E. Lewis (*Gun Crazy, The Big Combo*) was "completely unknown, a forgotten man" at the time Sarris mentioned him in *The American Cinema* (under "Expressive Esoterica"). Lewis told Sarris that this sudden late critical recognition made his life seem "worthwhile."

Would it have affected Herbert Leeds's fate if, instead of this blow, he had read what film historian Jeanine Basinger wrote about *Manila Calling* without any trace of inflation or special interest in his strange and obscure case? She starts by putting *Manila Calling* ("the prototypical WWII combat film") in good company, ("*Lost Patrol* remade first as *Badlands* and then as *Bataan*, *Manila Calling*, and *Sahara*.") Basinger rescues Leeds's film from oblivion in one stroke. Far from seeing it as a derivative work, she sees its "plot devices and characterization . . . later *[become]* staples of the combat genre. . . . However, the combat is guerilla effort, and *the presence of civilians removes it from the mainstream of the genre*" (my emphasis).

·   ·   ·

The idea of a character in a film ever being a mouthpiece for the director is even more suspect than in novels—unless the director wrote the screenplay. But there are limits to chance. In *Manila Calling*, there's an aristocratic European character who is a copy of my uncle in several ways: his flirting with suicide (he volunteers to "test" the water after Lloyd Nolan has wagered "odds on" that it is poison); he delivers a monologue about the world not being what it used to be, with which sentiments I believe my uncle, as an American raised in Europe and "sent to the best schools," would have concurred. He dies a brave death, manning the radio while explosions go off all around him.

·   ·   ·

When I offered Sarris a short précis of my uncle's life—his education in Switzerland, his knowledge of French (which led to his being sent to Quebec to direct *Five of a Kind*), his apprenticeship as a film cutter and editor and assistant director—he commented: "A lot of people who went to Hollywood were too good for Hollywood. Your uncle died too soon. Right before the idea of the auteur. He's the auteur that never was."

Our conversation ends with him heading off to see *Stone Cold*, "the kind of B movie that used to be ignored but which now has to be taken seriously."

Sarris has been ill. I wish him the best of health.

16

Why did my uncle choose to kill himself on his stepmother's birthday, May 15, 1954? I know nothing about the history of their relationship except what my mother has told me: that it was she, Tatiana, who suggested that Tarzan ask Jack Warner to give Bert a job (which he did); that they used to dance together in Europe when Bert was on vacation from school in Switzerland.

. . .

—Yes, my central informant has biases that could get in the way of complete objectivity; however, it is one thing to hear his kid sister claim he hated his stepmother, to be told that he chose her birthday, May 15, as the *Time to Kill* himself, out of . . . spite; but when you stand before the two gravestones and the incised numbers of her birth and his death blaze like a burning brand, you feel a chill you would not have imagined possible on a warm and sunny Sunday afternoon in April.

. . .

It is no mean hatred makes a man stick to a decision to die on one day— when as everyone knows, sun or rain, a chance meeting with a friend on the street, a cartoon, incongruous poster, or sight of some blessed eccentric walking a lobster on a leash, anything which—causes us to chance upon— the miracle of our limits—can lighten the bleakest mood, can lead—most anyone—to postpone—to hold off—to hold out—hope.

Just in case the next "heist," as every outlaw dreams, should set you up for life.

. . .

Why should he have hated her, she whom I loved?

My father also hated my step-grandmother, my Tat-Tat. (There are many dangers in this word "step.") He liked my grandfather and "took pity" on my mother but hated Tatiana. She, he claimed, was a witch. Never turn your back in her presence, he warned, or she'll stab you. She's evil, he said, over and over and over and over again. She picked out a trousseau for my mother and *charged it to him*. She had been a "kept woman" in Europe; he had her "dossier" compiled for the court during his divorce hearing. I never saw the fabled document, but that word "dossier" brought a chill to my spine.

(If I had not been born, her dossier would never have been compiled; she would have been spared the humiliation of the court case.)

The only malevolent images that come to mind when I think of her have to do with priorities. My mother claims that, when she wanted to call off her wedding to my father, Tatiana said it was too late because the invitations had already been sent out: this in spite of her loathing of my father—"Chaaales" as they called him, as if the "R" would remind them of his surname. She had bought lots of little girls' clothes in anticipation of her "grandaughter"'s arrival.

She did have one peculiar trait with regard to me: she insisted on calling me "Michael." And it gave her so much pleasure to say that name with its lift in the vowel and extra syllable that I was reluctant to correct her. Perhaps she was thinking of tough-fisted, cognac-drinking

MIKE SHAYNE

PRIVATE DETECTIVE

(In another Leeds film, *Just Off Broadway*, Mike Shayne is forced to share a hotel room with a fellow juror who asks, "Can I call you . . . Michael?")

Sitting at Tatiana's bedside shortly before she died, I noted a pile of *True Detective*s on the dresser. "You should read them," she said. "Bert always read the crime magazines. He was always looking for stories." (Everything with the very old and the very young is *always*. My little boy will even turn the word against itself and reward into punishment when he'll say, in protest, "well, you *always* want to buy me an ice cream cone.") Her faint smile was so beneficent when she said Bert's name I still find it hard to believe that she could have willfully wronged him. How Bert took her presence in his father's life, and as a possibly inadequate replacement for *the mother he never had*, is another matter.

As she lay dying, I sat holding her hand, and she smiled benignly (though not beatifically—that was not in her wily nature), and she told me what a good bedside manner I had and what a good doctor I would make and how I made her feel better than the doctors. When she finished this small soliloquy and grew tired, I asked her if she would like me to turn out the light and she said, "Yes . . . Mich . . . ael. . . ." This slip of the tongue forced me to consider that maybe she did not love me for who I was as much as she loved the image of me as a certain kind of young man that she had concocted in her fantasy, a "Michael" who would encounter the world with pluck and courage, like Mike Shayne. (Nor did it escape me even then that their doorman was a stocky ex-boxer named Mike.) As "boy" to Tarzan and "Mike" to her, I was slightly perplexed as to who I was for them; only slightly, because they couldn't have behaved more lovingly.

. . .

I wonder just how speckled and spectacular a past she did have before she met my grandfather. Had she "done everything," like my grandfather.

. . .

Tatiana once proudly announced that she had taken the ferry to Biarritz alone to smuggle dress designs from a rival company. (One try-on in the dressing room was enough for her to memorize the pattern.) In *Ferry to Biarritz* she stands on the deck in the mist, spray lashing her face, the belt of her raincoat drawn tight around her waist, her collar up over her ears, a faint enigmatic smile on her thin lips.

. . .

What else can I say against her?

She took me to movies I was too young to see.

Through childhood and adolescence I was haunted by the image of a man in a Hawaiian shirt with a bandaged chest, crawling through the treetops until, crouched beside a snowy TV screen in a ramshackle house outside New Haven, I saw the shirt and the taping scene toward the end of *From Here to Eternity*: Donna Reed ministering to Montgomery Clift's wounds. The part I had not remembered is that Prewitt is killed by his own men after the war is over.

Not long after I had this memory *firmly in place*, my father told me about the Sunday he went to see *From Here to Eternity*. He had come to get me at my mother's apartment, and she wouldn't let me out. "Devastated," plunged again into an unwilling solitude, he crept off to a matinee and the movie blew him away. Long after I heard my father's reminiscence, my mother let slip that my grandmother had taken me to see *From Here to Eternity* against her wishes.

I was "only four years old; it wasn't right. That was no movie for children."

After seeing *From Here to Eternity*, I longed to be wounded. My play fantasies were all of being wounded (but not killed by my own men)— I wanted my wounds to be wrapped in tape by a tender woman. Every time a kid drew a knife or grabbed some heavy object in a fight, I consoled myself with this image of a wound that would still leave me in pain, but functional, capable of loving and of being loved.

The other night, at dinner on a hill in Windham, someone asked what our favorite movie scenes were, and without thinking twice I saw a face in the leaves and the light sharp on that clean-cut face and the shadows of the leaves, the stark light-dark. I was surprised that it wasn't the scene from *From Here to Eternity* but the moment in Kurosawa's *High and Low* where we first see the kidnapper who has been holding an industrialist's son at high ransom throughout the body of the film; his face has the same weird innocence as Montgomery Clift's.

I begin to imagine myself, my mother's stepmother and my father seated before the same screen at the same Sunday matinee in Manhattan—and after I scribbled these fugitive notes this morning I notice that my handwriting made the acronym FHTE look like this:

FATE

17

People have always said that my handwriting is unreadable: while transcribing what I have written in my bound notebook about my uncle I notice that I type "My uncle lit up a room" when what I have written is "My uncle took up a lot of room: he was thickset, bulky, barrel-chested. He wore shades of brown: heavy tweeds. There was something suffocating about him."

The apartment on 58th and Park had the air of a hunting lodge. The medals and trophies, the signed photographs of Ike and Schweitzer, the embossed deluxe editions with blue-gold spines in the glass bookcase.

And many photographs of my uncle. A profile of him in his army uniform.

My mother says he was known as "the man who never smiled." I can see him in the smoky, overfurnished living room, gagging on memorabilia, seated across from my grandfather, leaning forward to make a point. The two burly men, equally vehement, were both leaning over to drive home a point at the same time. My grandfather scowling like a storm cloud.

Tarzan would later whine, "We were great pals, Bert and I. We did everything together. Everyone thought we were brothers."

There was only a twenty-year distance between father and son.

The father, a crack shot, teaches the son to become a crack shot.

The father, a champion amateur golfer, teaches the son to drill that gutta-percha ball over 250 yards into the foggy Scottish mornings; and the son, smashing a three-wood to "get home in two on a five hundred and sixty five yard par five," twists his knee on the wet turf; and his kid sister—there for a rare cameo appearance in her high-rolling brother's life—watches the youth's body go by on a white stretcher.

. . .

His second wife, Evelyn, complained to my mother that he liked to twirl his pearl-handled pistols to frighten her.

. . .

They were not self-obsessed, only action-obsessed. If there was no trouble around, they would manufacture it. While the two Jewish *Übermenschen* palled around together in Europe as "the net tightened" before the war, they went out of their way to frequent clubs and bars where Jews were verboten and beat the daylights out of anyone they could trick into making an antisemitic remark.

. . .

And yet Bert, already handsome, got a nose job and changed his name from Levy to Leeds in the Jew-run industry.

18

The copy of *The Return of the Cisco Kid* that arrives from Eddie Brandt's is clearly a copy of a copy of a copy. Though barely visible, it is quite audible, and I feel a shiver of recognition when I hear Cisco's first speech (recited with phonetic exaggeration in Warner Baxter's middling "Mexican" accent): "I am tired of Me-yi-ko. I dream of the blue mountains of Ar-re-so-na. It is a long time now since I breathe the cold air of the hills."

There are no guitars visible. Cisco has no sooner finished his confession of longing for Arizona's "blue hills" than he launches into "Down by the Old Hacienda" as he and his two sidekicks ride off, on the sawhorses they're sitting on to mimic the rocking rhythm of horses, into—not the painted desert—but the painted backdrop.

When I told one of my informants the story about Bert's refusal to shoot Cisco taking his guitar out of his saddlebag, he said that "every time they put a Mexican on the screen they wanted him to sing. But not Cisco. Cisco doesn't sing."

And yet not only does he sing, but at the end of *The Return of the Cisco Kid* he refuses a fistfight because he does not "use fists. If I hurt the hand I cannot play the guitar, and if I cannot sing love song I cannot make love, and if I cannot make love, I die."

What makes Cisco's yearning so believable? Is it that his longing is consonant with Bert's love of the West's open spaces? Or—blazing through the script's inevitable clichés—the pathos of its animating crisis: that the "heroine" cannot return Cisco's love—while appreciating the lifesaving favors he does for her father on account of her—because she could never, never—and how could he have thought it possible?—love the old man he has become, much less a Mexican?

Is it a cruel trick that the name of a suicide should be attached to the director of works called *Yesterday's Heroes*, *The Man Who Wouldn't Die*, and *Let's Live Again*?

Or does the oblique connection signal a—resurrection?

A rustling in the archives. The dust shaken from the "continuity" of *The Cisco Kid and the Lady*.

· · ·

I begin to see a certain malign, willful design at work. I'm off to Washington for a weekend spree with my son, and he has agreed, upon arrival, to go to the Library of Congress to screen *The Cisco Kid and the Lady*.

Our eyes linger wordlessly on the landscape, the endlessly multiplying signs, the constellation of boxcars and stone falcons, steeples and clouds;

the woman in black—jeans and turtleneck—except for a turquoise scarf with snails, who sits across the aisle, trying to find a nest for her Javanese puppets.

Between trips to the snack bar, people-watching, and gazing out the window, we recall the funny details, the absurd flourishes in *The Return of the Cisco Kid*, which we had watched in Windham on rainy nights at the end of August—like Cisco climbing out of his open grave after he has been executed because his pals had put blanks in the soldiers' guns.

Pals: "How do you feel to be killed?"
Cisco: "It deed not hurt one beet."

I'm really talking myself into looking forward to this, because I would much rather see *The Arizona Wildcat* or *Ride On, Vaquero* than *The Cisco Kid and the Lady*. One claustrophobic Western with the aging, wistful, melancholy Warner Baxter in the role of Cisco was enough. Mike Nevins had not yet written, in his synopsis of the series, that "*The Cisco Kid and the Lady* might better have been titled *The Cisco Kid and the Baby* . . . Cisco as usual falls for the woman in two seconds flat but claims the baby as 'his.'" Or that, with regard to another "Cisco" I had no desire to see, *Romance of the Rio Grande*, "a long forgotten actor named Ben Carter literally steals the picture in a small part as night watchman at the chief villain's bank . . . . [A]t a time when the deck was viciously stacked against people of color, he [Herbert Leeds] gave one black man his moment in the sun."

The title *Ride On, Vaquero* immediately brought to mind continuous action, a hero who was always departing, the thunder of horses' hooves pounding the ineradicable dust, and the new Cisco, the lean, swart, youthful Cesar Romero riding with the brim of his hat turned up against the wind.

.   .   .

Rosemary Hanes greets us. "You're here to see *The Return of the Cisco Kid* . . . and you weren't interested in *Bunco Squad*." I laugh: how many misunderstandings can multiply around such an empty center?

"No, I'm interested, but I've seen them. I want to see *The Cisco Kid and the Lady*."

"That's not what we have you down for."

"Would it be that hard to switch?"

"It's not a matter of that."

"What then?"

"We don't have *The Cisco Kid and the Lady*."

"_____"

"As I told you on the phone, we only have the continuity for *The Cisco Kid and the Lady*."

"Is that like the screenplay?"

"No, it's a record of what's actually filmed."

"You mean someone sits there and copies down what's thrown up there on the screen."

"Yes."

I hold the typescript in my hands and, in flipping through the pages, shake off the dust.

·   ·   ·

I content myself that I am finished, that I have gone as far as I can go, as I am willing to go, into my uncle's case, when Mike Nevins tells me I should try Boyd Majers at Videowest in Albuquerque to locate the Ciscos I have not seen. Boyd says he will send *Ride On, Vaquero* and *The Cisco Kid and the Lady* as soon as he "gets a check." I send it right away. Weeks pass, a month, two. I don't call because by not seeing them I will feel absolved from the possible banality of the films themselves. Finally, I call Boyd. "Yup. They're all ready. Have been for a while. They're sittin' here in a pile with all the others waitin' to be mailed." Boyd's leaning tower of Westerns . . .

Ride On, Vaquero and *The Cisco Kid and the Lady* make for painful viewing. Contra my fantasies, *Ride On, Vaquero* is essentially an indoor Western—even the outdoor ride through the desert at night is correspondingly dark. But many of the crowded indoor saloon scenes are composed like Renaissance paintings, which Bert had probably absorbed into his bloodstream during his adolescent years in Europe. Here in the midst of the most banal and predictable screenplay (no wonder he quarreled with Samuel G. Engel!) are compositions reminiscent of Murillo, Rembrandt, and Poussin, and the shots are never held longer than is necessary to propel the inertial action, the motor of the yawningly formulaic script, forward. The auteurists could recognize the brilliance in the flamboyant visual style of films like *Gun Crazy* and *Kiss Me Deadly*, but the art of Leeds's films is less obtrusive; it argues against the idea of the hero.

19

In *The Man Who Wouldn't Die*, Mike Shayne calls in Merlini the Great (Clayton Rawson's detective in *Footprints on the Ceiling*, not Brett Halli-day's from the actual Shayne stories) to consult "about magicians who are able to practice the art of shallow breathing." Merlini tips him off to the whereabouts of another magician, who is an adept at this art.

．　．　．

The magician in *The Man Who Wouldn't Die* has learned how to feign death, letting himself be buried in order to reappear as a ghost. He "dies" twice in the film. He is good for only one thing: not dying. Beyond this unique ability (previously mastered by Houdini and a few others) the magician has no character at all; he is his function.

20

The Mexican painter Rufino Tamayo died the other day at ninety-one. Michael Brenson, in his obit for the *New York Times*, noted that Tamayo's "passionate commitment to the craft of painting is unmistakable, as is his feeling for animals and fruit and for the ceremonial pleasures of play and dance."

You would think that it would go without saying that any significant art-ist would have a "passionate commitment to craft," but it is Brenson's way of not damning the dead entirely with faint praise. Tamayo was not a great painter but an exuberant spirit with terrific antennae, intuitions, impulses, generosity of heart. His paintings are saved from flatness and banality, from soporific single-mindedness, by one thing: the sun. Even the night, Brenson quotes Octavio Paz as saying, "is for Tamayo simply the sun carbonized."

Tamayo is a craftsman who became a significant artist almost by osmosis. He made the most of what he had. His gift grew with exercise.

Tamayo created one of the loveliest small museums in the world, in homage to solitude, in a house on a side street in Oaxaca. It's a museum you can breathe in—one that Robert Smithson might have liked. I went there in the rain and felt calmed as I watched the torrent pour through the open roof into the courtyard; I loved the way real life encroached on art as it always has on the great mound sites themselves. This art had to weather the elements. The Zapotec heat flows through Tamayo's brush. Tamayo stayed in touch with his sources. The closest parallel I can find to the Zapotec artists would be the Sienese: austere yet sensual, profitably ambivalent about figuration. Tamayo, like a succulent, drew what nourishment he could from the desert:

sun.

And this strikes me as being at the crux of what Herbert Leeds lost sight of: light. Herbert Leeds, who might have turned a corner and blossomed, held back—in the Blackstone Hotel.

It was shadows he honed in *Time to Kill*, not spot lighting.

21

I have always been wary of history. Reading the newspaper clippings that record my uncle's death I glimpse what may be the root of my suspicions.

Even as a small child, eager to be in my grandfather's company, it was possible to detect at least a trace of hyperbole, of embroidery, in this raconteur-boaster grandfather's recounting of his life and times.

And everything I can piece together about Bert shows that he, like the cops in *Bunco Squad* who are bent on breaking up the scams of fraudulent fortune-tellers, lusted for accuracy. But how to interpret Abraham T. Levy's relation to history, and to his own history in relation to history?

I think his larger-than-life life, his "wild game"—for he was a kind of life-artist who did back up some of his claims, as when he produced the article

Rube Goldberg wrote about him in the '30s—blew up into megalomania in his later years, and what this means, in relation to the truth, or the
facts, is that he put himself in the center of stories where his role was in all
likelihood peripheral. And there's evidence of this meddling even in the
information he gave the papers about his son.

These clippings are rife with contradictions.

Without for a moment underplaying the seismic effect of his son's death
on him, or his having been in shock, my grandfather unwittingly undermines my uncle by mentioning the films he didn't direct in such a way as
to obscure—to bury—the fine ones he did direct. This leads me to believe
that deep down the father did not honor the son's real contribution but
only his proximity to that which others deemed important. I have little
doubt that Bert knew this.

"Among others, his father said, he was one of the unit directors for James
Stewart and Debra Paget in 'Broken Arrow'; Tyrone Power and Patri-
cia Neal in 'Diplomatic Courier'"; and then, without transition, comes
the list of films he did direct: "John Emery and Hillary Brooke in 'Let's
Live Again'. . . ."

In naming pictures with "stars," like Stewart, Paget, and Power, was his
father thinking: *let those who will come later to the works of Leeds know that
in addition to the rapid, clean-cut films he did direct—whose names no one now
remembers—that he shot the action scenes for* Broken Arrow, *the first movie to
look at history from the Indians' point of view . . . ?*

.   .   .

The *Herald Tribune*, possibly through no fault of my grandfather's, has
Bert directing films which he merely edited: *The Life of Jimmy Dolan, The
Narrow Corner, I Loved a Woman*, and *Diplomatic Courier*.

His wife, Evelyn, from whom he was estranged, "told *Mirror* reporter
Sheilah Graham that the top-flight 'B' director's death *could not have been
brought on by financial worries*. He was well to do, and had an appointment
with one of the networks Tuesday to discuss a TV show." Yet the notice

in the *New York Herald Tribune* points out that he had "stayed first at the Beaux Arts for two weeks, and then had checked in at the Wyndham, April 4, paying $5 a day for the room." One can only assume he moved to the Wyndham because it was cheaper.

There is something disingenuous in my grandfather's statement that he "believed" Bert's death was an accident because he knew how to handle guns so well—"he was a crack shot"—and he learned his "gunmanship in the war." Hadn't the two "crack shots" often gone hunting together?

If Mike Shayne were addressing the jury, having vaulted from his seat in the jury box, as he does in *Just Off Broadway*, he might have asked—"And what else would he have been doing with a 20-gauge shotgun in his hotel room on this 'visit' to New York?"

His trick knee exempted him from army duty, but he would not be deterred and offered his services to the OSS. "I am not only a cameraman and crack shot, but my French is perfect and my German passable."

Bert's ability to shoot straight was another reason he was useful to the OSS. He could take a man out with one shot and not attract enemy fire.

Bert may not have performed any specifically heroic acts, but he was a durable invader—a triple threat: he could kill you, trick you, or take your picture.

As a Jewish officer, he may have felt more driven and committed than he ever had during civilian life. Like an avenging angel he would show the Nazis what the Jews were made of—and who knows but that, while he was hardly ever in contact with his mother after he left for Europe in his father's custody, it wasn't his mother's French-Alsatian blood crying out for retribution that made him so keen to return to Europe, to reach the front, and be on the bridge—taking photographs of men going off to their death with a tip of the hat—for the battle on which the war effort hinged. I think of his unit traveling all night through dark forests, spooked at times by the hooting of owls, and then arriving at the enemy night encampment just in time to catch them before they woke. The enemy stretches, turns over, thinks "I am dreaming" before they flush with anxiety at the reality of the cold steel of my uncle's bayonet at their throat. Or the popping of flashbulbs.

"According to his father," the *Herald Tribune* continues, "he was one of the two men on the Remagen Bridge spanning the Rhine when the Germans blew it up with mines, but escaped injury."

Only two men "on the Remagen Bridge"?

Was my grandfather empowered by such a thought as *who, other than my five-year-old grandson—whose future as a lawyer I have already begun to sow so that he should never be in want—would hang me up for saying Bert was "on the Remagen Bridge when the Germans blew it up with mines . . ."—so what if the bridge didn't fall into the Rhine in just that way, isn't it enough that my son's courage was never in question . . . ? I have, somewhere, the still photographs he took that day: you can almost hear the rivets popping. How can I find them now? Can't you see I'm blind?*

These literal people will be the death of me! I did everything for that boy. How could he do this to me?

.   .   .

The Remagen was a railroad bridge at a narrow point of the Rhine, and the Germans did all they could to keep the Allies back—but even ten days of steady shelling and attempts at detonation could not stop them from taking the bridge.

I've been wondering how he may have felt watching not only American soldiers go to their deaths but also many Germans who were hardly soldiers at all but civilians given weapons; that is, I'm willing to guess—not that there is ever a single incident that we can single out as signaling a downward spiral in the mind—that what he witnessed in his time at Remagen may have brought his mind to a dark place he could not escape after the war.

.   .   .

The detective's speculations, reported in the *Daily Mirror*, are the most believable part of the clippings. "Deputy Inspector Fred Lussen of the West
Side, theorized that Leeds put down a book he had been reading—and
which was found, still open, on the bathroom floor—loaded the shotgun
with a single shell, sat on the bed, and, holding the gun with the butt in
the air, fired. . . ."

.   .   .

This death, more expertly plotted than anything in his movies—with the
possible exception of the magician's shallow breathing in *The Man Who
Wouldn't Die*—shouldn't have been called a "suicide."

It was aesthetic homicide.

.   .   .

And it would be wrong to rule out that he didn't hate his stepmother
in proportion—perhaps unknown to himself—to how much he loved his
mother . . . despite the absence of any visible sign. . . .

.   .   .

But what, outside the boundaries of his misery, was his target? Did he
want to corrode what love remained between his father and stepmother so
he would blame her for his son's ruin? Or did he want to get him through
her and make it look like the reverse? From what I witnessed of their last
years I think it is clear where his "arrow" landed. . . .

.   .   .

The circumstances of my uncle's death remind me of one of Louis Malle's
somewhat cracked and beguiling early films, *The Fire Within*, which
chronicles its protagonist's last day—and daily round—before he shoots
himself. The book open on his desk is Fitzgerald's *Babylon Revisited*.

My uncle's last days, wandering Manhattan in a fog of depression, might
not have been so different from that of the enervated aristocrat whom

Maurice Ronet portrays in *The Fire Within*. He might have gone to a restaurant where he was once "known"; he might even have contacted a woman (as the Ronet character does—Jeanne Moreau) he once knew.

.   .   .

If I say in conversation that someone was "on the Remagen bridge," the listener might think I meant as well *in the area of the Remagen bridge*, within close range of danger but not perhaps sliding off the collapsing structure itself into the Rhine. Sometimes, as in the construction of a bridge, small details make all the difference.

.   .   .

Am I naïve (yes) to think (yes) that the papers might have tried to corroborate the facts—just to let my uncle die with a little dignity.

.   .   .

I can see my grandfather's terror mounting as he dialed the number over and over and over to get Bert to walk across the street to celebrate Tatiana's birthday and heard the desk clerk utter the heartbreaking words, "I'm sorry, Mr. Levy. There's no answer," and, because he feared that something terrible was about to happen even though he may not have known he feared it at the time, called Brigadier Munson, who lived in the penthouse apartment at the Wyndham to go and knock on Bert's door. And so it was Munson, "his close friend," who first saw the "sign written in crayon, on a sheet of hotel stationery, and attached to the door of Mr. Leeds' third-floor room [which] said: 'Maid. Do Not Disturb.'" It was Munson who "let himself into the room with a passkey obtained from the hotel clerk."

.   .   .

What if my grandfather lied? My grandfather's lies did not kill my uncle—they merely added to the pathetic ironies. His lies magnified what he did not do—that he did not direct *Broken Arrow* and the other A pictures that were listed or direct the stars headlined in the obit. My point is simply that the truth might have emphasized just how good the work he did was—

for though he worked on what was known as "Poverty Row," his films do not look impoverished. *The Man Who Wouldn't Die* and *Time to Kill*, with their sweeping chiaroscuro, are small classics of the genre, precursors of film noir.

My uncle had a way of having shadows and reflections precede or comment on a scene, as though this were the real understated theme: that our deepest intentions are somewhere noted—if not in spoken words or visible actions. These moments are slipped into the hectic nonstop flow so quickly it would be easy to miss them if you weren't looking for them. Like four-leaf clovers. But they're the artist's signature. They show there is something more than words and actions in a world of words and actions. They point to the limitations of "facts." The shadows make his films more haunting than if there had been ghosts, and not merely magicians who can hold their breath for an hour when buried alive.

22

Why should Abraham T. Levy have broken with the parable of Abraham and Isaac, even if his namesake and remote forefather had a motivation that came from on high?

Of the many paintings that render this story, one by Domenichino illustrates much of what is unsayable, unknowable about what happened between Abraham and Isaac: here they are almost skipping, father and son—almost running toward the hilltop to keep their appointment, their robes flung out toward the precipice, the kindling strapped to the boy's back like a quiver, Abraham's outstretched hand aimed toward the altar in the clearing where God's emissary rides a cloud through the stand of trees over Abraham's shoulder—as if answering for the rachitic twinge we still feel in the scapula where we once had wings.

Could Abraham have asked, *What am I doing*? Could Isaac have taken his eyes off the knife and squirmed free or in some indefinable way resisted? Or should I be satisfied that Isaac read his father's inner gaze, took in his ambivalence about the sacrifice which he could not, would not, express on his face.

Isaac on the chopping block—offered up—for what? For the good of generations, the general good? The invisible bond is the more binding one: it is Abraham who cannot meet Isaac's eyes. The narrative torments human history—which gasps in the wake of Abraham's compliance. Of Isaac's compliance. Abraham's hand too steady. Too free. Isaac a too willing collaborator in his own demise, asking no conditions of the hill or the urgent conditions of the journey.

"Father's Wild Game"

I might never have heard my grandfather's story of his adventure on the Staten Island ferry if I hadn't been wearing white socks. How can I forget that day when, as in a speeded up film, so many things came together? The money I had earned throughout the summer working as an envelope licker at my father's office was burning a hole in my pocket. I had to buy something for my grandmother. It would be different from any other little gift I'd bought her because this was money I had earned. I passed a street vendor selling jeweled handbags for ten bucks. Who could resist? She'd probably think it cost twenty, and even if she never used it (when would she get out of bed?) she would get the idea: that I cared for her. It was, I think, a June afternoon, a perfect New York pollution cocktail: just the right degree of heat and humidity to mix with the fumes to make you think you were sniffing glue from a paper bag. A great day!

I arrived. Tarzan let me in. Stared. Hugged me gleefully. Tatiana dragged into the living room dressed—though she no longer left the house—in a navy blue suit with a gray sash across it, seamed stockings, blunt, open-toed shoes.

I presented her with the glittering bag. She cast her eyes over it. I knew she knew it was junk and wondered what possessed me in the first place . . . what was wrong with flowers? (Too temporary for my taste—but then I was giving the present.) "Thank you very much, dear," she said, with no trace of insincerity. "It's a lovely bag, Michael, but I don't want you spending money on me. You should save your money and not spend it. Where did you get this bag?" My pulse quickened. What did she suspect? She'd handed it to Tarzan, who must have felt its chintziness: the roughness of the fabric, the jaggedness of the rhinestones.

"It was on sale at Bloomingdale's," I lied.

"Dear," she said with a reserved tone she rarely used, "I asked you where you got the bag."

"At Bloomingdale's."

"You did not get this bag at Bloomingdale's, dear."

"All right, I'll take it back."

I was glad that Tarzan could not see me blushing.

"You're sure no one gave it to you?"

"No." I was exceedingly nervous—what was she getting at?

"I said I'd take it back."

"Take the bag back, dear, and save your money. Don't buy me presents. And don't ever buy a woman anything personal, like perfume or . . . a handbag."

Did she understand that this stupid present was only a token of the enormity of my love for her? What else could I buy her other—other than flowers—or chocolates?

The fixity of her expression unnerved me. Gone was the faint smile that usually accompanied her gaze when she looked me up and down.

"Are you still going to the Luxor Baths with your father?"

"Huh?"

"Is that why you're wearing white socks?"

I looked down at my gray cuffed chinos and white socks.

"Huh."

White socks? Had I missed something? This was "standard male attire" in my high school in Salt Lake City. Everyone, from the greasers to the clean-cut kids, wore white socks.

"Do me a favor, Michael, and don't wear white socks."

"Why?"

"Because that's what all the fagelas wear. That's how they tell each other apart."

After she finished her diatribe, Tarzan, who had been exceptionally quiet, asked me if I ever saw "Chaaales" consorting with other men at the Luxor Baths, the gym he often took me to after work when I was with him in New York. I thought of the characters who inhabited the steam room, scrotal sacs dangling immensely between protuberant bellies and skinny legs; mavens of the ovens, who, like firemen in a reversal of roles, hurled bucket after bucket on the rocks to increase the production of heat. And the glum comedian who broke deadpan with a mock silent scream only when some ancient eternal presence of the steam poured a bucket of cold water on his head.

Then he asked me, in the same quiet tone he used on the phone, if I "liked fairies." I felt a surge of complicated outrage. "No," I said, wanting to put an end to this discussion. "Well, I wasn't implying that you were one . . . but if you're going to the baths with Chaaales, you're bound to meet them."

My early life as a teenager in Salt Lake City did not exactly prepare me to take note of the codes of this homosexual underworld.

Tarzan's cheekbones tightened, and he spoke in a cool and measured tone I had only heard when he mentioned my father's name. "I met a fairy on the ferry," he began, and that opening made me bite my lip. His tone was too solemn for the alliteration. "I was on the Staten Island ferry in broad daylight." An artful raconteur, he paused to give me time to take in the image: two people on the world of an immense deck, glitter of water.

"I was standing at the guard rail watching the waves and the light on the water when something brushed my elbow. We were alone on the deck and this . . . guy"—he gave the word the same emphasis and gravity as *Chaaales* to underscore the presence of something sinister and insidious—"stood right next to me." "Listen to your Pop Pop," Tatiana chimed in, as though this were my one-shot lifetime inoculation from the threat of homosexual advances. . . .

I listened. I was used to his hysterics, but this quiet, even, measured tone really scared me. Tarzan continued in his hushed tones that were at the very least respectful of the existence of evil. "I said, 'Excuse me,' hoping he'd go away. And then he mumbled something, the way they do, something foul and disgusting, and I turned to him and said, 'If you say another word, I'm going—to kill you.'" I imagined he was reproducing the same steely look he used that day. "I don't know what the little fairy was thinking, but he repeated it. I couldn't believe my ears. So I hit him." He demonstrated his right cross. "And knocked him clear across the deck." I thrilled to visualize a punch of such velocity. (Why, whenever I slugged someone, did my knuckles go into mourning for days on end?) "He wiped his lips and smiled and said something else about . . . sucking . . . and then I lost control. I pummeled that fairy. I had him against the rail and I beat that fairy into a bloody pulp. There was nothing left of him. And as he lay gasping on the deck, one of the crew came over and asked what happened. I told him. And you know what he said?" Did I want to know? "You should've killed that fairy."

While I was awestruck by his stories of beating up antisemites—proof that not all Jews were weaklings—this was merely brutal, excessive, and unnecessary.

"So I picked that fairy up by the lapels and said, 'Next time I'll really kill you.'"

I wanted to ask what he was doing in Staten Island that afternoon.

I wanted to know why the memory was so alive for him.

"So Michael," Tatiana chimed in the moment he finished his tale, "no more white socks."

.   .   .

My last attempt to reach Tarzan by phone in the hospital room where he lay dying was a perilous event and one he would have appreciated. I had walked out to the phone booth under the unimpeachable enamel of a November sky in Arizona. Two boys were waiting ahead of me. The one already using the phone was a sturdy surfer from (where else?) southern California. He was about my height (six feet) and weight (165 pounds) but better myelinated. He talked on and on in hushed intimate tones, once in a while pausing to brush back his bangs, cut fashionably just above his eyebrows. He wore another uniform in which I could never fit: tan khakis and penny loafers without socks. The other boy was handsome, short-haired, freckled, and tall even by standards of the West (around six-foot-six). I had never seen him around the campus before. He remarked that I looked "downcast." I told him it might be the last time I would talk to my grandfather. He didn't say anything. Several minutes passed. "Are you about done?" he asked the surfer. The surfer nodded and waved him off. Several more minutes passed. "How long are you going to be?" the tall boy asked again politely. The surfer did not look up but waved his hand as it to say, "All right, all right, stop rushing me," and turned his back to rid himself of this heckler, this nudnick. The tall boy moved like lightning, spun the surfer around by the shoulders, hung up the phone for him, and said with at least a dram of humor in his voice, "I guess you're done now." "Get your hands off me," the surfer replied and pushed the tall boy against the wall. The surfer's sullen look quickly turned to shock when the tall boy grabbed him by the shoulders and slammed him against the wall again and again, and within seconds a look of utter terror sprang onto the surfer's face. The tall boy was possessed. He handled the surfer like a toothpick. I had never seen anyone react so quickly, with no transition between his standing silently by and this high-speed violent pummeling. (It had the suddenness of Michael Whalen jack-in-the-boxing Leon Ames after his escape from the closet in *Island in the Sky* (Leeds, 1938) or the moment in *Pickup on South Street* when Richard Kiley captures Richard Widmark in the subway with a flying tackle. . . . The bad guy doesn't even get a chance to look up.)

The fact that the surfer was now dating one of my ex-girlfriends did not prejudice me against him (we had separated amicably, and the two were similar in every way given certain stock gender differences). I neither liked nor disliked him, though he'd seemed complacent and self-satisfied; and while he may have needed to be "shaken up," this humiliating attack, reducing him to a whimper and a kind of "yes sir, I'll do anything you tell me to do now, sir" attitude, seemed far beyond what was called for, and I pitied him as he slunk away.

"I won't be long," the tall boy said, the red retreating from his freckled cheeks as quickly as it had appeared. "By the way, my name's Ward." He held out his hand. "Pleased to meet you," he said.

Ward waited while I called New York. The hospital switchboard connected me to my grandfather's room.

"Hello."

"Hi Pop. It's me. Mark."

"I'm glad you called, boy."

I could tell he didn't have his teeth in his mouth. That, amid the small sounds of his sobbing, rendered me numb.

"I'm not going to make it, boy. This is the last time we'll talk."

"I'm sorry, Pop."

I was so choked up I could barely croak out—"I love you."

"I love you too. It's all right. I did it all, boy."

"I know, Pop."

"Goodbye"—I could hear him fumbling with the phone—"son . . ." Had the attendants arrived—or was this the very paraphernalia of death I heard rustling like static? And then someone hung up the phone. *Why are the dying so peremptory?*

.   .   .

Ward and I became great friends. I found his story mysterious. I don't remember if there was one reason (such as being thrown out of school or knocking up his girlfriend) why Ward had left Davenport, Iowa, and come to complete his senior year at Judson, but he had a certain consistent self-destructive pattern that was connected to his behavior in the phone booth. It was temper, yes, but something more than temper. It was something that pervaded his being all the time.

.   .   .

Ward had the potential to be an all-state basketball player and was considered the best juvenile amateur golfer in his state. He was chosen to play Arnold Palmer in an exhibition match and claimed to have outdriven Palmer by twenty yards on every hole with his Black Widow driver—which had a forty-four-inch shaft. You had to be Ward's height to swing it, and if you could keep it from hitting the ground before it reached the ball, you could gain extra height and distance, thirty to forty yards per drive.

Ward's problem off the tee was control. His short game was terrible. He was reduced to idiocy once his drive landed him within a hundred yards of the hole. He'd scuff an approach shot and yell "Hit it!" at himself. If his next shot stopped short of the green, he'd yell "Moron!" "Jesus mother fucker Christ!" He'd whack the ground with his short iron or his putter. The earth reverberated.

.   .   .

My grandfather initiated Bert and then me into the mysteries of golf. When my moment came, he took out the wooden-shafted clubs he'd had custom-made—*sculpted*—in Scotland. They were placed in a black leather bag. "When I die, boy, these will be yours. Try and lift them." I could, barely. The bag itself weighed at least fifty pounds. "How do you think my caddie felt?" The fact that nobody played with wooden shafts anymore didn't seem to bother him. "And my shotguns. Gable offered me ten thousand dollars for these guns. It'll all be yours, boy." Then he took me for a walk around the block. The nearest bookstore conveniently turned up a copy of Tommy Armour's classic *A Round of Golf*, and the nearby sporting goods store, Korvette's, was plentifully stocked with drivers. It was out of the question that he should buy me a set of clubs.

We meandered over to Central Park. There were still some patches of snow on the ground. He took off his overcoat and draped it on a bench. Still fully dressed in his navy blue suede wing-tips and heavy tweed jacket, shirt and tie, he gripped his wolf's-head cane and assumed the stance he had taken some thirty years before and showed me his graceful, even swing. It looked a little like Doug Sanders's swing, a swing that would fit inside a telephone booth. "You don't have to bring the club back all the way. What matters is the speed of your hands at the point of contact. It's all"—he wagged the club head—"in the wrists." He took a few swings. For a seventy-five-year-old blind man, he had terrific range of motion and balance. "Do this for a few years before you ever hit a ball," he said.

The right grip, the right stance—I could hardly get my two hands around his wrists. My own wrists and hands were slender, like my father's. I took a few swings, jabbing the clubface clumsily into the mud. "For the love-a-God," he said, instantly discouraged. "I just showed you. Follow through." "I guess I'm used to baseball, Pop," I said, in a weak voice.

"He thought he was a great teacher," my mother said later. She told me that when Tarzan took her out for a tennis lesson, he would smash the ball as hard as he could at her face and copious breasts and then get angry when she couldn't return it. When she complained about the velocity of his slams, he'd say, "Protect yourself with the racket, Margy."

Tarzan possessed an inscrutable sadistic innocence. He proudly told of how as a boy he would pitch steaming fastballs all afternoon at his brother, and when he saw the pain on his face it made him pitch harder.

We all desperately wanted his love, his approval. People who inspire this in us are *the most dangerous people in the world.*

.   .   .

When I was a little boy, he taught me how to box by making me hit his hard outstretched palms barehanded as hard as I could. I don't think he intended cruelty. Boxing, for him, was a form of nurturing. He'd sit there in one of his bulky tweed jackets, the silk handkerchief overflowing the breast pocket, with a bemused expression. He could move his hands out of the way faster than I could hit them and when I landed a punch on his granitic biceps—it hurt my knuckles. It wasn't the sport that frustrated me but how seriously he took it. My feelings were of no account: this was the "manly art" and I had better damn well master it. I didn't. Instead, I contracted a horror of physical violence.

.   .   .

Tarzan's golfing stories were his best. In his description of his rounds with Walter Hagen and Tommy Armour, he evoked a world of order and gentility. For him, these golfers were first of all *gentlemen*, gentle-men. Since Tarzan was a *bid*nessman and didn't have time to practice, he perfected his swing. He could easily outdrive Hagen and Armour. Putting was his weak spot.

But lest you think me credulous in believing that my grandfather was all that he said he was and could outdrive these legendary golfers, I assure you that I have concrete evidence of his prowess. One evening, as dusk filled the windows of their smoky apartment, Tatiana appeared with the crinkly yellowed clipping of an article from the *International Herald Tribune* from sometime in the '30s. The creases ran deep as an old treasure map. "Your Pop-Pop was the French Amateur golf champion." I had heard this claim made many times—but here was proof: an article by Rube Goldberg (prefaced with a sketch of Rube contorted within one of his own contraptions)

about all the things Tarzan "talked and talked" about, including his victory
in the French open, shooting a 59 to win. "A fifty-nine!" I exclaimed, as-
tounded. I had never heard of Hogan or Palmer shooting such a low score.
"Oh my God," he said, in his thunderstruck voice, as if I had questioned
the veracity of his claims. "It wasn't a par-seventy-two course," he assured
me. "It wasn't a par seventy-two," Tatiana chimed in, "but your Pop-Pop
did win the tournament."

He told of matches with heavy betting, of one in particular in Scotland
where he was a hole behind in match play as they approached the eigh-
teenth tee. He couldn't win the match—the best he could do was tie. "I'll
bet you double or nothing that I can cut the dogleg," which would mean
hitting the gutta-percha ball over a high stand of trees, some 250 yards in
the air. He made this offer to his opponent, a rich businessman who, even
with his "handicap," saw fit to liberally improve his lie in the rough and
shave a stroke here and there. " 'You're on,' Mr. So-and-So said, calling
my bluff. 'Laddie,' my caddie said, though he was a good deal older than
me, 'no one has ever driven the ball over those trees before.' It was a cold
afternoon; in fact it was beginning to snow, and the ball doesn't fly as far
in the cold." Tarzan was heavily in debt. "So-and-So would have trusted
me for the money, but that wasn't the point."
"How did you stand the pressure?"
"Well, I tell ya, boy. Da noives. Concentration. That was the key." Demonstrates with cane how he addressed the ball: firm stance, iron grip,
eagle-eyed gaze. "I smashed it toward the trees like a rifle shot which kept
rising until it vanished, barely clearing the topmost branches. I confess I
was relieved when we found it on the fairway."

.   .   .

In spite of the fact that he had grown up in Montclair, New Jersey, and
spent much of his life in Europe, New York accents had crept into his
speech, not with everything he said, just the words he laid a heavy stress
on like "noives" and "detoigents."

(He blamed his blindness on a fall from a horse on a mountain trail at Leo
Carillo's ranch. His horse jammed him against the abraded rock face and

"Pancho" could not save him. That "set loose" his cataracts. He told the story over and over, always beginning "it all started—.")

He would finish reading the paper, no mean feat for a blind man. Then he'd rise and smash his palm against his forehead. "What's the matter," I'd ask, dreading the answer. "The detoigents are killing the fish . . . the soap suds . . ." His response to issues of the earth was utterly visceral. He'd shudder, and a dark look would cross his face and distort his features as he involuntarily clenched and unclenched his fist. "For the love of God," he'd mutter gravely as the breath left him. (He said "fortheloveofGod" so often that it had become one word.) Now he'd be raving, yet choked up with rage, on the brink of tears. "For twenty five years I've been talking the detoigents." To whom, I wondered. Who do you talk to about these things? "I told Javits—the detoigents are killing the fish." He'd walk to the sink. "Suds. You see these suds? You don't need these suds to clean. But people think suds make things cleaner. So I said, 'Where will the suds go?' And they said, 'Into the river,' and I said, 'There you have it,' and they said, 'What?' And I said, 'For the love a' God.' No one listened. Did you know that I invented the deodorant thirty years ago? But I wouldn't market it because it closed up the pores. The pores have to breathe. What do you think happens to the sweat if it doesn't come out? Don't ever put anything on your body that keeps you from sweating. A fragrance is all right, but no antiperspirants."

Did I need further convincing?

I loved him for his passionate response to life and longed to comfort him. Now when he said "boy" in a slightly hoarse and muffled tone, I could see that he was remembering in his body his own boyhood. In a way his hysteria, verging on megalomania—his overdramatization of ordinary life—was the natural response, given his belief that every human action had a deep effect on everything around it.

.   .   .

Once, before he died, when I had become a passable golfer, I told him I'd shot an 80-something. He said, "A *real* eighty? Or did you move the ball if you had a bad lie." "Well," I said, "these public courses aren't in great condition." "How many gimmees?" "Only tap-ins," I said. "But some of them were, I bet, about this far," and he held out his hands wider and wider. "I guess so," I said. "Well when I shot an eighty," he said, "it was a real eighty."

Out came the "waterproof" woolen sweater he'd had made in order to play golf in the rain in Scotland. It fit me like a glove. I wore it steadily for twenty years, at which point the collar and sleeves began to unravel, and I am still unable to find the magic wool with which to repair it.

. . .

Every so often I got to visit my grandfather's office, the one that housed his perfume business, Parfum Lorlé: the quiet; the green carpeting; the golfing trophies; the glass bottles of cologne displayed in glass cases; the limey scent of "Hole-in-One," its plastic golf-ball-shaped top adorned with his initials "A.T.L," for Abraham Tarzan Levy. Moving through the hush, past the back offices, their doors slightly ajar, I could see no evidence of work, just the thick, burly backs of the brothers in their oak swivel chairs talking on the phone, quietly. There were no papers scattered on the desk, no *disarray*, no hustle-bustle. They were always *too happy* to see me. "Come"—this was the first priority—"let's say hello to Mr. ——" And then a perplexed-looking geriatric case would rise and emerge from the shadows in the corridor looking for cues as to how to behave. I would shake hands with him, a slender, hoarse-voiced man with wobbly jowls. Tarzan would whisper, "Mr. —— is a very fine gentleman," which translated into someone who wouldn't cross him.

My uncle Sam, Tarzan's brother and partner, would rise slowly from his chair, as if fighting not only gravity but distraction, reverie perhaps (though I doubt that)—perhaps the heaviness of his woolen jacket—and greet me with something less than enthusiasm. "Hi . . . iii . . . son," he'd drone. What an effort it cost him to say hello! He would hug me, lethargically, noncommittally. Sam was the John Cage of monosyllables. He rarely spoke but could say "yeah" in a hundred ways. His deep bass voice edged toward a growl. His "yea—hs" leaned toward pentameter. I could hear a ticking sound in his throat. Had he swallowed a clock? I liked Sam, but his phlegmatic behavior confused me. (It never occurred to me as a child that he was simply dull.) Though handsome in his way, he had no affect. Tarzan made the money and spent it; Sam tallied the gains and saved it. He wouldn't even reimburse Tarzan for money he spent entertaining.

. . .

Family businesses. The flamboyant figure always loses. Tarzan was not in business to make money but to support his habits, subsidize his interests. Sam was only in business to make money.

Tarzan never bad-mouthed Sam, merely expressed his sometimes vicious glee at his dominance over his brother. Tarzan did everything better than Sam. Except that Sam was not reduced to filling Chivas Regal bottles with B & L scotch or pulling Garcia Vega wrappers on stogies (try doing this when you're blind) he bought for five dollars a box. But he performed these acts gleefully: "People only care about labels. They can't taste the difference." Only he, known in the perfume business as "The Nose," could have done that! (Both my father and my grandfather died with precisely the same—realistic—fear of destitution.)

But Tarzan could say, imbuing the simplest sentence with an ingenious pacing and voice tone, "Your uncle Sam is coming over later to say hello," in such a way that we would both burst out laughing.

He could laugh at himself too. When I told him he looked like Donald Duck in a navy blue smoking jacket with a white belt and white lapels that someone had given him, he exploded with such childish glee—I could tell he loved me all the more for the jibe.

. . .

When Tatiana died, the brothers sat across the darkened room from each other. Sam clicked his tongue and wagged his head—to show mournful feelings I suppose. Maybe it was a brotherhood made in heaven; maybe Sam did all the dirty work while Tarzan had all the dinners. If Tarzan hadn't died when he did, he wouldn't have had enough money to live more than another two years. Sam died, I'm told, a millionaire.

The Night

I

*S*ummer. 1993. The worst heat wave in living memory. I lie awake all night, night after night, in Windham, Vermont, thinking about the flood-waters of biblical proportions sweeping across Kansas and Missouri—the Mississippi swollen, bursting the levees, the farmers eyeing their drowned fields from National Guard helicopters.

I go downstairs and pace the two-hundred-year-old rented farmhouse, stare out the windows and wait for the deer. Torn between ecstasy and exhaustion in the gray of dawn, any thoughts I might have had about a split between the mind and the body are destroyed in this insomniac state.

I had despaired of how to begin an essay on Michelangelo Antonioni until another long night of sleeplessness threw me a line.

I thought of Monica Vitti's rapt gaze when she looks up as the wind strums the stark white flagpoles against the blackest sky, and of the couples in the trilogy *L'Avventura*, *La Notte*, and *L'Eclisse* and the photographer in *Blow-Up*, who stay up all night. It is only in this fragile, indeterminate state that we can begin to see for ourselves the presence of the world that Antonioni's films relentlessly present.

The pure fact of the world. The egalitarian nature of the sensual world.

Why the night? Stay up through the night and you come to the end of something. Something that is disappearing.

. . .

At that time I slept very little; I'd adopted the habit of going to bed as soon as the day's gradual fade-in began. ("Toward the Frontier") *

2

The work of the most demanding artist of the stellar group of directors to emerge in the 1950s seems to be in eclipse. *The Passenger* was the only film of Antonioni's to be shown commercially since *Zabriskie Point*. He could not get his late films distributed or made. *Identification of a Woman* never opened in America after its screening at the New York Film Festival. *The Crew*, which intensifies Antonioni's focus on the Third World, was never shot. Neither was *Technically Sweet*, his most ambitious screenplay, though many of its themes were absorbed into *The Passenger*. And yet the reputations of his somewhat more literary contemporaries, such as Bergman and Kurosawa, have, if anything, grown in the past two decades.

. . .

On my way to the retrospective of his work at the Walter Reade Theater I could not help but note that a building under demolition across from the café looked like a three-tiered jungle ruin: the exposed floors, the steel cables sprouting everywhere like vines. The air was heavy with an almost paralyzing humidity.

And each day there was less of the site, though by the time I arrived, mostly in the late afternoon, there was no sign that the wrecking ball had been at work. Just dust and silence and the hovering presence of the ruin.

I would not mention this building being leveled had it not brought to mind the most riveting scene in *I Vinti* (The Defeated), in which, to escape his pursuers, a man on the run descends the scaffold of a construction site, going endlessly down and down, as if the planks and ladders had no bottom, and we switch from thinking about his escaping the other men to his escaping this dark labyrinth. Physics has sprouted a metaphysics.

*All quotes not otherwise identified are taken from interviews with Antonioni or his prose—especially *That Bowling Alley on the Tiber: Tales of a Director*, translated by William Arrowsmith.

· · ·

There were screenings for his early films at 10:00 A.M., and one time I went with my friend Rachel Hadas to see *La Signora Senza Camelie*. We arrived anxiously, as one does at such events, and struggled to be on time, because even if there is no one there, or just two or three desultory souls (who nevertheless take up a lot of room) scattered throughout the theater, the projectionist will run the film at the appointed time. Still, it is a shock to see only two or three people in the theater (do "film people" have such easy access to the cosmic archives that they can see what they need to see when they want to see it, when amateurs like myself are forced to bend their schedules to fit the screening time . . . ?).

3

The process of creation is notoriously difficult to record on film. Writing, music, painting: all resist being captured by a machine which renders only outward appearance. As Antonioni stated in an interview: "Film is not image: landscape, posture, gesture. But rather an indissoluble whole extended over a duration of its own that saturates it and determines its very essence."

That process is most evident in *Blow-Up*, in which Antonioni uses photography, the least metaphorical of all the arts, to define the human condition. He takes his cue from ancient sources and quotes these remarkable lines of Lucretius: "Nothing appears as it should in a world where nothing is certain. The *only thing certain is the existence of a secret violence that makes everything uncertain*" (my emphasis).

From the moment *Blow-Up* opens, the photographer, Thomas, seeks that which is missing, the disappearing center. After spending the night taking photographs in the flophouse for the homeless, he is too wound up to sleep; and after asking that his clothes be burned—shaving, half-dressed in his white jeans and wide black belt, while his gofers attend upon his eagerness to leave—he dons the last part of his outfit, an emblem of his youth and high spirits, a midnight-blue velvet blazer, and makes his way toward a park where he revives, comes alive like a young colt. Storming the steps, "relaxed and payin' attention" (as the line from the Byrds' song from that time has it), he enters a garden (one of paradise's false trapdoors) and proceeds calmly, in full control, ready to receive the image: the mystery is ready to offer itself to him.

Antonioni wonderfully depicts the restless waiting, the fever that precedes creation. Thomas is frustrated by the ease with which he can control the finite realm of his work and still feel there is a fragile bond, at best a truce, between what the naked eye sees and reality. Once at work, he is focused, intent: fully alive. Alone in his darkroom he blows up a seemingly innocent, yet suspicious, photograph—again and again until a gun can be made out, and it is not long till it's clear that it's pointing at a dead man. But as he goes on looking (as the camera pans back and forth between him and the photograph on the wall), enlarging the image, it decomposes.

·   ·   ·

Disappearance is the normal order of things for Antonioni.

"People disappear every day," The Girl in *The Passenger* says.
"Every time they leave the room," Locke replies.

·   ·   ·

And the strange thing is that there's a vague sense of guilt at the back of my conscience, I feel it flowering like a shadow, a Hitchcock-like shadow of doubt that falls on the coherence of my life. ("Report about Myself")

·   ·   ·

Blow-Up returns over and over to Thomas's photographs of the disinherited, the homeless; they are part of the larger puzzle he is trying to assemble, along with the death of love between himself and his wife and the escapism of the woman in the antique shop who wants to get out of herself and find renewal in Nepal (to whom Thomas replies, wittily and wearily, "Nepal is all antiques").

Thomas comes to understand in the course of the film's slippery dialectics of appearance and reality, that he is one of the disinherited—that what separates him from the men in his photographs is economics. His camera has recorded something that his sensibility could not register. By uncovering the "secret violence" that appears before him in the darkroom, he begins to learn how to live inside manifold contradictions. To exist—even as he is implicated.

4

It is in direct apposition to dailiness that Antonioni fastened on the night-long vigil as a way of opening his characters' eyes. Sleeplessness awakens them to their animal nature: it peels away the folds of ego, pretense, identity. What remains is a naked eye that sees the alien strangeness of the familiar world.

. . .

The beautiful and terrible moment before dawn when the gray light signals the sky's *clair-obscur* resistance. . . . There is a shagginess to this hour that I love.

The trees fill with wind; expand. And the all-night vigil prepares the way for the eye to see. The blindness of a sleepless night lays down the path for sight; insight—duration's timeless time.

Last night, in the long-awaited thunderstorm, it was like driving under water, and it reminded me of two scenes in Antonioni's films that have that "terrible beauty": the scene in *Identification of a Woman* where the headlights can make no further headway in the fog and there is no self or other in the wetness that encompasses the lens, and the scene in *L'Eclisse* in which Vittoria and Piero watch the "dire spectacle of the wrack" of Piero's car, driven into an artificial lake by a drunk, rise from the dark water with its headlights on, casting a ghostly trail.

. . .

The night, during which Vittoria and Piero get acquainted, prepares the ground for their rendezvous at the intersection the next afternoon. They do not appear, but the camera does and, in a seven-minute crescendo—a

Waiting for Godot with objects as characters—renders the independence of the world apart from an individual point of view. The sequence provides an escape, a break from the problem of other minds; a resolution, not a solution.

> *. . . the director's problem is that of embracing a reality that ripens and consumes itself, and to set forth this movement, this reaching a point and then advancing, as fresh perception.*

.   .   .

In the tense, nightlong lover's quarrel which comprises the first scene of *L'Eclisse*, Vittoria keeps going to the window, from which she sees the wind blowing through the stark black trees and the fiercely alien mushroom shape of what I take to be a water tower. (This suggestion of a "mushroom cloud" comes back in the form of a headline warning of nuclear threat in the final sequence.) Then the camera moves outside the house for the first time, and we see Vittoria suddenly dwarfed by the black trees nearest the house as they lean toward her, embodying the full range of the terrible and the beautiful.

.   .   .

It is not the trees and water towers that grow stark and gigantic in the night but our senses that are awakened. Our working lives prevent us from indulging in the night.

I pause, having taken up this essay when the temperature was rising, to listen to the wind in the trees and see if it spells some relief. . . .

5

The world Antonioni renders means something very specific to him. He deploys his art as one way of crossing "over the border of the purely physical without knowing it."

> So spoke of the existence of things,
>
> An unmanageable pantheon

Absolute, they say
Arid.

A city of corporations

Glassed
In dreams

And images—

And the pure joy
Of the mineral fact

Tho it is impenetrable

As the world, if it is matter

Is impenetrable.

—George Oppen

More a filmmaker of place than of objects, Antonioni has gone so far as to color smoke and paint trees so that places in his films would be expressive of his character's inner crises. He took this to an extreme in *Red Desert*, where yellow, factory-waste smoke insults the sky and chemicals mar the blue-green Adriatic off the coast of Ravenna. "There's something terrible about reality," Giuliana tellingly remarks, "and I don't know what."

. . .

Antonioni is an investigator, a diagnostician of social ills. His devotion to uncovering the truth, peeling away the layers of his characters' self-protective armor, is a laborious, tense-making activity. His work cuts against the grain of modern life, which turns its back on time and duration and sees itself cut off from the past.

Perhaps Antonioni had to hit bottom and make *Il Grido*, with its dour portrait in gray—in which the characters are truly in the landscape and in the grip of labor conditions in the Po Valley in winter ten years after the war—before he could in good conscience alter his focus from the social to the existential. I mean literally hit bottom—as the protagonist, Aldo (played by the sluggish American actor Steve Cochran), hurls himself from a tower, and for a moment his agonized cry scorches the air.

. . .

The form that "secret violence" takes is also—death.

In addition to the suicides of Rosetta in *Le Amiche* and Aldo in *Il Grido*, there is the death of Giovanni's best friend in *La Notte*; the death of a stockbroker (who was given "a minute of silence" broken by the antiphonal ringing of the phones) in *L'Eclisse*; the murder in *Blow-Up*; the question of whether or not Mark killed a cop in *Zabriskie Point*; Robertson's death in *The Passenger* (which enables Locke to assume his identity). All these are deaths about which no one cares enough, but they are deaths which galvanize action—and force the living to confront their lives.

Learning how to live is necessarily learning how to mourn.

6

Antonioni's films became more and more rarefied as he came to locate, to focus on, to *blow up*, to explode, the timeless human problems as signified by a title like *Identification of a Woman*. The lives of characters freed from "the practical restraints which imprison him or her" allowed him a more intense focus on the conflicts that lie underneath the social matrices, or the "cover" of work.

Antonioni has always been incisive where matters of class are concerned and nowhere more prominently than in the early films in the neorealist vein. Consider the nightclub scene in *Cronaca di un Amore* where Guido, tense, sweating, as if flames were about to shoot out from the crown of his skull, looks on as Paola—the ultimate object of his desire, the rich girl, pursuit of whom is his raison d'etre—carries on in a flippant fashion, bedecked in jewels and a ludicrous, absurd "leo-leopard" hat.

7

Profession: Reporter. Antonioni started out as a journalist, film critic, and documentary filmmaker and always approaches filmmaking as a kind of investigation. Part of his task is to give an account of certain conditions. Watching his characters try to live their lives against a background of modern verticals and horizontals that show no love for human scale, we understand why he envisions his work as digging: "archaeological research among the arid material of our times." His worldliness, his awareness of history have given him the freedom to leave it out and look more closely at the human dilemma of living after the Second World War.

.   .   .

"The sun is fierce up in these hills," writes another chronicler of those years, Cesare Pavese (whose novel *Tra Donna Sole* [*Among Women Only*] Antonioni adapted as *Le Amiche* [*The Girl Friends*]). "I had forgotten how its light is flung back off the bare patches of volcanic rock. Here the heat doesn't so much come down from the sky as rise up underfoot—from the earth, from the trench between the vines which seems to have devoured each speck of green and turned it to stem."

Antonioni's films, in addition to his adaptation of Pavese's novel, reflect Pavese's tone: his obsession with real time and the feeling of being, as he phrased it in his diary, "alone, alone, alone."

For Pavese, who committed suicide shortly after receiving the Strega Prize for *Among Women Only*, only others had life. He was undone by the problem of other minds. In one revealing diary entry he wrote: "6th January 1946. Gods, for you, are *the others*, individuals who are self-sufficient, supreme, seen from the outside."

Pavese makes you compliant in his quest: he offers an invitation to wandering, saying, come on, let's go into the hills, it's cool, it's clear, and we can look back at the town and get things back into perspective. There's the long, slow ascent, the careful deciphering of paths from natural openings in the brush that don't go far enough, the blend of solitude and dialogue (if accompanied by a friend), self-abandonment, all tied to the ascent; then the melancholy turn homeward and the more thoughtful, darker descent, as the perspective gained from the height is lost again.

But sometimes Pavese did not want to come down. He did not want to sacrifice possibility—which seems endless when you look down at the town from far away—for the probability that he would return to the old ways when he reentered the town walls. In town, among others, he felt lonely. In the hills, alone, he felt—for a moment at least—the joy of solitude. A moment, a split second, of solidarity with the world.

. . .

Antonioni takes this quest for perspective a step further. His characters have a lust for altitude: they "get high" by taking to the air. In *L'Eclisse*, Antonioni reveals Vittoria's capacity for elation as she enjoys her ride as a passenger in a small plane—a digression that conveys what it feels like to fly better than any film footage I've seen, as if we were experiencing it from the point of view of the plane itself. Daria and Mark "communicate best" in *Zabriskie Point* while he flies a plane over her car in the azure air in slow, teasing, twisting, erotic circles against a backdrop of mountain, mesa, and the whiteness of the desert.

. . .

> How do you know but ev'ry Bird that cuts the airy way,
> Is an immense world of delight, clos'd by your senses five?
>
> —William Blake

. . .

Antonioni was inevitably drawn to the character who is the embodiment of "professional" entrapment: "Locke" in *The Passenger* (originally titled *Profession: Reporter*). Not that Locke (Jack Nicholson)—in a segment excised from the final cut and handed out with the director's approval in the retrospective "packet" under the title of "The Reporter You Never Saw"—isn't aware of how different things could be. "Yeah, it's strange how you remember some things and forget others. *If we suddenly remembered everything we'd forgotten, and forgot everything we usually remember, we'd be totally different people*" (my emphasis).

There is no escape from the desire to escape.

Antonioni is nothing if not restless; he loves to let his camera pick up the other "stories" that appear around the edges of the story. Or to find oblique and eerie ways of detailing the inner states of his characters. Niccolo, the blocked director in *Identification of a Woman*, dreams of escaping to the sun. In the bravura coda, Antonioni shoots his spaceship—made of minerals able to withstand millions of degrees of heat—voyaging into the savage red.

Antonioni's endings break free of what precedes them, like rockets sprung loose from their boosters. And his characters fight against their animality, but they cannot escape (not even "to Nepal"). In *Profession: Reporter*, the uncut version of *The Passenger*, when Locke and The Girl repair to a garden, he grows quickly restless in paradise and says, "Let's go eat. The old me is getting hungry."

8

It is no small task to convey the experience of transcendence on film: in *L'Aventurra*, Antonioni builds up to it in the uninhabited town under construction, the nowhere before they reach Noto, where Claudia and Sandro wander between ancient arches in the roughy whiteness—drying out the spirit.

"It isn't a town, it's a cemetery."
"They designed it like a stage set."
"Once they had centuries of life, now—twenty years."

The nun who leads them up to the bell tower in Noto has never ascended to that physical height before even though she lives right below it. When Claudia (Monica Vitti) accidentally touches the bell rope on the tower, it sets all the bells in the ancient city ringing out in response to her love: they answer her call.

Sandro is an architect who has abandoned aspiration for commercial success—and whose life is hell on account of it, a fact which strikes with shocking force when, having come down from the tower, he knocks over a bottle of ink "accidentally on purpose" by letting his keys swing to and fro until the inevitable occurs, and he destroys an architecture student's sketch. Inevitable, too, is the way the student, not yet crippled by a life of waffling, flies at his throat. It is the energy of this student that Antonioni will gravitate toward in the future when his love affair with Monica Vitta comes to an end.

I go among the Fields and catch a glimpse of a Stoat or a fieldmouse peeping out of the withered grass—the creature hath a purpose and his eyes are bright with it. I go amongst the buildings of a city and I see a man hurrying along—to what? the creature hath a purpose and his eyes are bright with it. . . . May there not be superior beings amused with any graceful, though instinctive attitude my mind m[a]y fall into, as I am intertained with the alertness of a Stoat or the anxiety of a Deer? Though a quarrel in the Streets is a thing to be hated, the energies displayed in it are fine; the commonest Man shows a grace in his quarrel—By a superior being our reasoning[s] may take the same tone—though erroneous they may be fine—This is the very thing in which consists poetry. . . . (John Keats)

.   .   .

Even Locke (now Robertson) has a moment of delirious freedom when he simulates flight, leaning from the funicular out over the blue waters of Barcelona harbor. But ecstasy exacts its price. In the next scene, as Locke waits in the park in Barcelona for his first rendezvous with the cipher "Daisy," he meets a winsome yet curmudgeonly old man who sees the children playing as his springboard for this pessimistic reflection: *other people look at the children and they imagine a new world but he just sees the same old tragedy begin all over again.*

These sentiments recur in Locke's bleak parable at the end of *The Passenger*: a man who has been blind all his life is so disturbed by what he sees when he gains his sight, the dust, the ugliness, the repetition, that he kills himself.

.   .   .

Antonioni is trying to discover what mutations in the character of his characters have been brought about by change in the world. "The milieu . . . accelerates the personality's breakdown . . . [but] it isn't the milieu that gives birth to the breakdown; it only makes it show. One may think that outside of this milieu, there is no breakdown. But that's not true."

9

Seeing has been the central metaphor of Western culture ever since Oedipus plucked out his eyes. Or ever since Freud fashioned his "complex" out of that singular action.

The art of film is not only well suited but may have been created, in an evolutionary sense, to get this paradox of sight out in the open. Sight, where moving pictures are concerned, requires the dimension of time, and this is where mainstream cinema most often relinquishes its claim as art. Antonioni is among the few directors who have had the courage to experiment with real time in long takes, phrased and framed within a context in which there is at least a trace of a story. He has sought "a cinema free as painting which has reached abstraction . . . a cinematic poem with rhyme." Time passes. Duration is timeless; it exists out of time. "Only through time can time be conquered," wrote Antonioni's favorite modern poet, T. S. Eliot.

.   .   .

Antonioni devoted a sketch to Eliot in *That Bowling Alley on the Tiber*.

> *"Who is the third who walks always beside you?"*
> "When a line of poetry becomes a feeling, it's not difficult to put it into a film. This line of Eliot has often tempted me. He gives me no peace, that third who walks always beside you."

.   .   .

Antonioni resisted the bastardization of montage into shock-effect, "Mabusian" audience control, knowing that the time was propitious to go the other way, to get back to and rediscover the origins of an art that had developed, from a technical point of view, too quickly for its own good.

> I believe I've managed to strip myself bare, to liberate myself from the many unnecessary formal techniques . . . of much useless technical baggage, eliminating all the logical transitions, all those connective links between sequences where one sequence served as a springboard for the one that followed. The reason I did this was that I believe . . . that *cinema today should be tied to the truth rather than to logic.* (my emphasis)

In place of controlling the emotional reaction of the viewer with a cut, Antonioni holds the take until a trace of true feeling can come through, as he phrases it, in "a world where those traces have been buried to make way for sentiments of convenience and appearance: a world where feelings have been 'public-relationized.' "

10

Antonioni exhibited a series of paintings, blown-up gouaches really, in Rome in the early 1980s, called *The Enchanted Mountain*; and while I found myself unable to respond much to the work, the sequence clearly alluded to Cézanne's method of painting the same mountain again and again; which is how, in his long takes, Antonioni lets time fan out, expand, and flower in a scene so that truths imperceptible to the naked eye can be perceived. In film he has sought to hold the retinal focus until duration enters the work of its own accord. For his paintings he magnified the initial "image" a thousand times.

. . .

Not concentration on the "thing" but on the scene.

(And what did Antonioni do in the short documentary *Return to Lisca Bianca* if not, to the bewilderment of the crew, make everyone sweat out a hot July morning on the island and wait until noon for two clouds to provide some shadow-play before saying yes to Take One.)

The fact of a secret violence that throws everything in an uncertain light is what we come to after an hour on the treeless, rocky island of Lisca Bianca, searching for Anna, the disappearing center of *L'Avventura*, who has been reading *Tender Is the Night*. (This "dis-appearance" is Antonioni's concession to plot mechanics—akin to Hitchcock's MacGuffins.) The starkness of the rocks on the island; the steady pulse of waves broken once by a cataract that rushes up and scare-thrills Claudia; the high, direct sun, forcing everyone to squint and screen their eyes to keep the glare from blinding them; the elemental otherness of this wild outcropping of stone in contrast to what awaits them on land.

Is there something sinister or menacing about the universe? Something more—than indifference? Or is it that people are often flummoxed by the curve balls, change-ups, and sliders that life throws them? Life is lethal; ambiguity the poison of choice.

.   .   .

There is a stillness that takes place in the interstices of volcanic activity.

> The black donkeys move single file down the narrow lane,
> hooves striking sparks on the stones,
> while magnesium flares answer back from obscure peaks.
>
> —Eugenio Montale, "News from Mount Amiata"
> (my translation)

Antonioni's work is perched on an active volcano: it registers the seismographic shock of the scene in Rossellini's earlier *Journey to Italy* when, on a visit to Vesuvius, Ingrid Bergman and George Sanders come upon a man and a woman who, while making love, were buried in the lava flow that leveled Naples.

Sandro remains too mired in melancholy to respond to Claudia's joy. He embodies the dangers of professionalism. Which ignores the night. He's the "new man"—and a new kind of character for Antonioni to use.

In successive films, Antonioni identifies the architect, the stockbroker, the writer, the photographer, the reporter. And then a woman—who is two women.

The architect is a paradigm of the larger human problems: how to address life, to stay in touch with the violence underlying change, rather than making something that is merely the mirror of the time. And postwar Italy is a place, as Montale has it in "News from Mount Amiata," of "fragile architectures."

Sandro's character is an instance of how you do yourself no good in the long run by scaling down your ambition, artistic or spiritual, to make your life more frictionless in passage through this world.

. . .

The "novelist" Giovanni (Marcello Mastroianni) in *La Notte* is similarly trapped in his (glum) idea of what it is to be a writer (like a Moravia character adrift in a novel by Pavese).

Having emerged from the womb of his room only to attend his own book party, he moves looking out of place and bewildered for the rest of the day and through the night.

He notices that Valentina (Monica Vitti) happens to be reading Hermann Broch's somewhat obscure modernist classic, *The Sleepwalkers*. This makes her climactic line even more pungent: "I'm not intelligent, just wide awake."

The night allows the truth to slip in, or slip out, as in the final scene toward dawn when Lidia (Jeanne Moreau) reads Giovanni a love letter that he, ghost of himself that he is, thinks is beautiful beyond measure, unaware that it was he who had written it.

In the lyric moment that concludes this sequence, Valentina tells the numbed couple that they have "exhausted" her, and then she stands, quietly alone, silhouetted in the doorway, right knee slightly bent, black hair and dress in stark contrast to the whiteness of her skin, and turns out the light.

. . .

If there is a central weakness in Antonioni's ouevre it is that his male leads are rarely adequate to the complex parts he would have them play. He needed characters like the architecture student, in whom the animal was still alive.

After the dissolution of his offscreen relationship with Monica Vitti, Antonioni moved his focus away from women to raw youths, like David Hemmings in *Blow-Up* and the streetwise non-actor Mark Frechette in *Zabriskie Point*, who could move like kinetic and magnetic cursors through his meditative films.

11

The quiet of the night awakens our sensitivity to sound-images that we are normally too preoccupied to attend.

In Antonioni's films you are never free from sounds. In the first scene in *L'Eclisse* the loudness of the fan—which encroaches on the room, oppresses the room like a praying mantis—is played off against the susurration of the wind in the bushes. At the end of the scene the slamming of the gate reiterates the finality of the man's departure.

And at the "press screening" of *The Passenger* to open the retrospective, which Antonioni attends with Maria Schneider on his arm, the propeller fan in the first scene whirrs like an infernal machine; whirrs so loudly I think there's something wrong with the projector.

In *Blow-Up* the soundtrack replays the sound of the wind in the trees (which I suspect has some very personal root in the etiology of Antonioni's imagination) that accompanied the first stage of Thomas's discovery.

It is not the first time Antonioni puts wind on the soundtrack where there could be no such sound in the room.

12

> The sensation I have when I feel that it's the shrilling of the telephone wires in the country that makes the landscape impatient. Especially in the first days of spring, when you hear more.
>   I think of this impatience transferred to people, peasant families for instance. It's not true that peasants are patient. And I think of the crisscrossing of the telegrams in those lines, with all their stories. And a soundtrack based on that shrilling. . . . ("The First Days of Spring")

Antonioni looks at people—not objectively, not independent of any point of view, but to investigate how they interact with objects. And to underscore how human development lags pitifully behind technology.

Technos grows. People talk to each other face-to-face less and less.

Mechanical objects are monsters of repetition. Niccolo can't get the burglar alarm his ex-wife has installed to stop ringing.

Gadgets multiply, like the child's robot in *Red Desert* which beats its head repeatedly against the wall.

.   .   .

During the showing at the Walter Reade Theater of his early documentary about the workers on the Po river, *Gente del Po*, a tear appears in the screen. The bulb behind it blazes like the streetlight at the end of *L'Eclisse*.

And all I can do is stare at the hole in the screen, the rip in the fabric, the light that cuts through the masts of the barges as they set off down the Po.

13

There are no long nights without an element of boredom. And boredom is an essential component of Antonioni's work. The problem of boredom is inseparable from the problem of time. Antonioni's use of time is the closest analogue I can think of to the use of time in the works of Faulkner, Joyce, Proust, Woolf, and Broch (more in his sentence-long novel *The Death of Virgil* than in *The Sleepwalkers*). This has to do with the ramifications of duration—moments of perception which take consciousness a long time to detail, to populate. Consciousness can never unravel all that it perceives happening in an instant.

Any inquisition into the nature of time is doomed to the use of paradoxes, analogies, which are doomed to imprecision. You're always running up against a wall of intervening space.

That means it's time to buy something: it's easy, satisfying, and only begins to exert an inertial pull after it has been possessed, like the guitar Thomas tosses into the street after working so hard to wrest it from others at the Yardbirds concert.

14

The night and time. Things get fuzzy when you talk about time. Science is still in the process of discovering the intermittences that the body knows. "Intermittences of the heart," as Proust phrased it in his search.

.   .   .

At the end of August a slight breeze sets off a clicking in the dry weeds. Driving back roads, I note the change in the attitude of nature when it's further from the highway or well-trafficked route: fences step out of shadows, and the curvatures in the hills let you see them in more detail. This is a landscape whose language is a fructive dialogue between wilderness and settlement. And yet I sense there is something perilous in the spaces between the cultivated and the wild.

I walk into the woods at nightfall, down a path I have not taken before. I walk a while, begin to feel my way and notice it is darker than when I set out. Ten, fifteen minutes have passed. The darker it grows, the clearer it seems that I am walking through a tunnel, that the trees have been here so long their topmost branches touch, intertwine; and the tunnel looks like it is narrowing, but it is the absence of light that makes it look like there is less space ahead.

Only now do I note that it is (once again) darker than when I last registered the change in light as light. This is what I remember best about the walk, and it occupied maybe ten seconds out of half an hour's meander.

This is close to where duration is positioned in relation to time. Duration exists in time, yet it is hard to imagine it separately from space. Duration is time as it curves into space.

The artist who lets himself be pursued by duration risks, in defeating time, defeating the tension necessary to make the work live. You believe in moments out of time, Eliot's "moment in the rose garden," or you do not. The latter row is easier to hoe. The sensualist argues against timelessness. Duration occurs in time but feels subjectively like it is out of time. In time you're coterminous with yourself. In duration, you're walking beside yourself.

Once I look back, and the entire path's in shadow. I realize I have to gauge my progress by the sky.

Shadows put a matte finish on the path.

What is infinite about this silence if I am in the act of hearing it?

15

While boredom is not necessarily a component of music or the visual arts, I can't imagine literature in some degree without it—with the singular exception of lyric poetry, which destroys as it conflates the dimension of time. (That time is not a factor in, say, a sonnet is one reason why the form is so adept at arguing that nothing will outlast its "powerful" rhymes.)

Antonioni has staked his claim as an artist. I remain confounded as to why people who admit to having no problem with the boredom factor in such works as the *Iliad*, the confessions of St. Augustine and Rousseau, the *Prelude*, Tolstoy's novels, and the numerous more ambitious works of the modernists, object to what is a precondition of Antonioni's long takes. They are the cinematic analogue to Proust's way of touching on the rush of images that flooded Marcel's sensorium.

Antonioni knows how to release the tension of a long take and release it powerfully—as when Lidia in *La Notte*, in flight from the breezy hospital room where Tomasso lies dying, walks fearlessly (scaring a man who stares at her) through the outskirts of Milan and comes across the boys who shoot off rockets in a field and talk of reaching the moon. A phallic chant goes up: "Terrific thrust!" This thrusting off into outer space is congruent with Antonioni's avowed desire to be in on the action and catch a ride up there as soon as possible: Kennedy, just prior to his assasination, had granted him permission to participate in a space flight.

I'll admit that the scene at the stock market in *L'Eclisse*, a riff on gambling, is a little too long; but how do we know that it does not shrewdly set the tone for the scene that follows—Vittoria watches an elderly man who has just lost a fortune, proceed, stoically and matter-of-factly, to the pharmacy for a tranquilizer and down it quietly at an outdoor café, with no visible sign of grief—to have maximum impact.

. . .

It's a risk to fashion an art that shows people in a shiftless, distracted, uneasy state; between the acts, in the mess. And yet to show them killing time in this state of anxious uncertainty is to show them at their most human—which doesn't mean that members of the anxious audience would recognize themselves in these portraits.

Antonioni is after truth, not proof; diagnosis of the problem, not a cure for symptoms.

He is the artist of the peripheries, for whom the only center is that which does not exist (except to disappear, like Anna and the victim's body in *Blow-Up*). The periphery is the realm of the possible.

> It's . . . the sort of film I've always wanted to make and have never been able to, *a mechanism not of facts but of moments that recount the hidden tensions of those facts, as blossoms reveal the tensions of a tree*. . . . [I]t was one of those evenings controlled by invisible looks. In short, an unexpressed tragedy. *The characters in a tragedy, the places, the air one breathes—these are sometimes more fascinating than the tragedy itself, the moments preceding tragedy and those that follow it, when the action is firm and speech falls silent.* Tragic action itself makes me uneasy. It's abnormal, excessive, shameless. It ought never to be performed in the presence of witnesses. In both reality and fiction it excludes me. (my emphasis)

. . .

Film is a hybrid, an admixture of all the arts that preceded it. Antonioni's use of these materials is ascetic—no empty virtuosity: technique has always been the servant of necessity. By the time of *The Passenger* in 1975 he no longer wanted to "employ the subjective camera, in other words the camera that represents the viewpoint of the character." After Locke's death the camera, as if weary of confinement, wants to look outward again. What does Antonioni do when confronted with what had hitherto been thought of as a technical impossibility? In the final scene of *The Passenger*, which consists of one long take, he had his crew cut through the window bars of the hotel in Osuna so that the camera could see further, emerge, look back at the scene it had just shot.

When asked in a filmed interview with Lino Micciche, *Antonioni as Seen by Antonioni*, shown for the first time in America during the retrospective, "Does the camera have a future?" Antonioni, still spry and youthful in his seventies, did not hesitate to answer: "It will."

POSTSCRIPT:
Noto–Mandorli–Vulcano–Stromboli–Carnevale

As if to echo the ending of an Antonioni film, I had no sooner "completed" this essay than a friend lent me a documentary that Antonioni made in 1991—a film that deftly amalgamates many disparate themes that circulate throughout his work. It is an ecstatic (yet lucid in that ecstasy) meditation on terror and beauty. The benign and the malevolent are married everywhere in this deft ten-minute imagist/cubist tone poem.

The film is as relentless in its own way as D. H. Lawrence's contrapuntal "Bare Almond-Trees":

Have you a strange electric sensitiveness in your steel tips?
Do you feel the air for electric influences
Like some strange magnetic apparatus?
Do you take in messages, in some strange code,
From heaven's wolfish, wandering electricity, that prowls constantly around Etna?

· · ·

Noto. Synthesizer bells and bird songs. The faces of gargoyles, which range from the beatific to the loutish. The female gargoyles gaze upward like aspiring angels; the males leer from the balconies. These gargoyles are brutish but shrewd: not moral. They indicate that the human conception of what it is to be human has not changed so much over the years.

> He reacts, he loves, he hates, he suffers under the sway of moral forces and myths, which today, when we are at the threshold of reaching the moon, should not be the same as those that prevailed at the time of Homer but nevertheless are.

The meditation on their expressions links up with the carnival masks at the end of the film. And they bring to mind the coarse faces in the stock market scenes in *L'Eclisse*, where it is easy to mistake the human lust for activity with greed.

Mandorli. There is nothing terrible about the blossoming almond tree in this segment as it fills the lens. Only the world surrounding it is terrible. And yet this Edenic moment, like the grove that Locke and The Girl enter in *Profession: Reporter*, owes everything to history, violence, and chaos.

Vulcano-Stromboli. The volcanoes come as an interruption but they are in themselves interruptions. Volcanoes are populated. They are not at the core; they are the core. As children we pretended that molten lava flowed between the volcanoes of our adjacent cots. We wrestled. And the loser would be dissolved in the infrared flow.

I have walked the cracked, sulfurous lava crusts on the island of Hawaii where several thousand small earthquakes occur every day; and while they don't shake you up, you pick up the activity in your nerves, and it is not unpleasant—because it is real—because it is an inviolable seismographic reminder that life is fragile, robust, dangerous; a reminder that just because you can't see something doesn't mean it isn't there, like the murder in *Blow-Up* which the camera—more sentient than the man who wields it, yet without any moral authority—records.

.   .   .

Antonioni is asking us to ask: what can be done with information? Can I act on a received image? *I*? Vittoria can transform herself after looking at some photographs of lions at home in the bush in Africa, but can lions react to photographs of us? Can lions be deceived by images, like Stevens's men eating images of themselves?

How else explain the force of distraction in Antonioni's films? The volcano is a silent witness to history, to the explosions of news and eros.

In most films violence is erotic, often delicate to the point of being balletic in execution: that is part of its allure. With Antonioni sex and violence occur with volcanic force, as when Guido comes under the spell of the nymphomaniac in *La Notte*, or Rachel Locke's feral boyfriend crowds her in *The Passenger*.

And there is always Mount Aetna, brooding over Claudia's hesitant caress of Sandro in the last shot of *L'Aventurra*.

· · ·

Volcanoes: female when they smoke; male when they erupt.

· · ·

The camera approaches the crater slowly, circling, trying out various approaches. The volcano changes with every new angle. The gorgeous green-gray verges on the comforting, like the park in *Blow-Up* that looked so "peaceful and still" to the photographer even as a murder was being committed. Murder and death are allied within the seething center here.

The camera does wonderful things with the craters; they're ridged; entry is blocked. Sulfurous fumes rise continually from the vents around the rims. A hovering precedes descent. Bare, barren. Curvaceous. The lens caresses the black igneous rock, revealing now a whale's hump, now the concave look of a sarcophagus. Everything has a double life: the steam around the craters' rims recalls the deus ex machina "fires of hell" at the end of *Faust* and the refining fires which the lovers pass through in *The Magic Flute*.

Gradually a center is revealed, steaming on all sides. Closer and closer the camera moves toward the heat at the center.

I am violent by nature. A doctor told me so when I was a boy. And I must give vent to this violence one way or the other.

.   .   .

Carnevale. The grotesquerie is not to be taken lightly. The masks are vastly less ambiguous than the gargoyles. There is something inexorable about the slow, mechanical movement of the shark's jaws as it bites the empty air; and the tinsel-breathing, lean, intent face of the dragon grows ferocious in its glittering. Time does not move on the charming, feline papier-mâché clock faces.

These shots marry the heat of the volcanic cones and this reflected light that then—in a quick cut—blazes as a sunflower, with lights strung along all of its paper petals, like steam rising from the rims of craters. Like light on light, reminiscent of the final shot of *L'Eclisse*: a close-up of light itself, energy in radiant form. And yet the center of the sunflower is dark. . . .

.   .   .

Night is threatened. It is not what it used to be. The night is what we can see of the volcanoes: a night that offers no repose is terrible. It is an incendiary night, about to burst into flames,

> Either now or tomorrow or the day after that.
>
> —Wallace Stevens

Once again, silently, definitively here, an inquiry into perception.

Catastrophe Practice

> What meaning would our whole being possess if it were not this—
> that in us the will to truth becomes conscious of itself as a problem?
> —Friedrich Wilhelm Nietzsche, quoted as an epigraph to *Judith*

I

Hopeful Monsters is the final installment in Nicholas Mosley's *Catastrophe Practice* series; it was preceded by *Catastrophe Practice, Imago Bird, Serpent*, and *Judith*. Although Mosley is the author of eighteen volumes and one of the best writers in English since the Second World War, he is best known in the United States as the son of Oswald Mosley, the founder and leader of the Fascist Party in Britain, whom he portrays with compassion and fairness in his autobiographical biography, *Rules of the Game/Beyond the Pale: Memoir of Sir Oswald Mosley and Family*.

Throughout the *Catastrophe Practice* series, Mosley fights against his father's central flaw—his willingness to embrace fixed ideas while managing to miss the point. This is a point of maximal tension for Nicholas Mosley: the only false moments in his work are when he tends to overcompensate for his father's misdeeds by sometimes embracing what he scorned a little too fervently. The elder Mosley, like the Nazis, saw Nietzsche's superman as an actor rather than an active intelligence, a literal figure and not a (hopeful!) metaphor and, like the Nazis, he was guilty of the same willful misreading.

My father assumed that Nietzsche was using words as recommendations about how in practice things should be arranged: whereas Nietzsche for the most part himself seemed to say he was talking ironically: he was using words to describe people's hopes and illusions about how things should be arranged and just by this—the recognition of people's capacities for illusion—perhaps not to be trapped by them. Nietzsche's superman is someone who hopes by seeing people's struggles for power and their capacities to delude themselves about these, to have some power over himself; not, in any way except this, to have power over others. (*Beyond the Pale*)

"The will to truth" that Nietzsche insisted on is precisely what Mosley's father and other leader types of the early twentieth century (several of whom make cameo appearances in *Hopeful Monsters*) lacked. As if to counterbalance their single-mindedness, Nicholas Mosley's characters grapple restlessly and relentlessly with contradictions and paradoxes, the limitations of language, and people's capacity for hope and ability to change.

> At the beginning of *Catastrophe Practice* there are characters on a stage: they are saying—Look, here are old patterns; they are to do with antagonism; they are likely to blow us up. We can't get out of old patterns by willing to do this: this would be to impose just one more falsity. *But by the experience of seeing that this is so we will in some sense be out of old patterns: by demonstrating this to an audience, might we be scattering seeds on the ground in which they can grow?* (my emphasis; 1988 "Postscript" to *Catastrophe Practice*)

Mosley's quest is to understand the forces of change. In the process he examines and "revalues"—without trivializing—some of the ideas that were central to Nietzsche, Wittgenstein, Heisenberg, Einstein, Mendel, Lamarck, and Heidegger. In this series he adopts catastrophe theory—a mathematical model that describes "how, in life, things work in sudden jumps, as opposed to how they work with simple matter which is smoothly" (*Imago Bird*)—as a unifying construct. The energy released in a catastrophe has an unpredictable effect; it can go in any direction, depending, to some unknown degree, on its environment. In Mosley's model, birth, death, the theory of relativity, mutations, all play prominent roles.

2

Nicholas Mosley's method, fusing Nietzsche's jousting epigrammatic style with narrative drive, has evolved to where it can accommodate *Hopeful Monsters'* bold mixture of synapses and adventure, autonomous fantasy and scientific treatise.

> I went skiing. I was on my own. I was in southern Germany. In the moun-
> tains there were these shapes, bumps, curves, that I sped down. I thought—
> All right, yes, these slopes are like that image of the pitted inner surface of a
> sphere: the four-dimensional space-time continuum of the universe. Such an
> image might not be a metaphor for scientific reality. . . . (*Hopeful Monsters*)

But there are also physiological roots for Mosley's method: it is intimately
connected to his stammering, which he lends to Charlie in *Accident* and
to Bert in *Imago Bird*. In his autobiography he sees it as "the indeed often
ludicrous outward sign of an inward contradiction; it is as if the sufferer
were half conscious of having swallowed paradoxes as if they were some
snake." Mosley cannot tell a story because there is never *a* story; the interruptions are what interest him. He wants to track the orbits of thought,
each of which constitutes its own stab at the truth. Because language,
within his rigorously epistemological practice, is never more than a "shot
at reality," the reflexive consciousness possible within a work of fiction sets
him free.

> It seemed to me that novels might be a way out of using words by which
> one could not only set out what one saw of life but by this *see the way in
> which one saw*; and through this, because it was to do with not being trapped
> by life, something might change. What usually happened with words was
> that people argued in a straight line; and then it was as if after all the curve
> of space brought them back to the beginning, and nothing changed. (My
> emphasis; *Beyond the Pale*)

Mosley's stammer, in addition to being a reaction to his orator father,
was also his unconscious way of repairing one-dimensional interpretations
of reality. Stammerers stammer because they can't render what is in the
mind—the larger picture, lost unity—in sequential speech. The stammerer
has not repressed the awareness of how little of what comes out "for all its
lovely cadences (perhaps because of them?)" has to do with "what is going
on in one's head."

The sense of lost wholeness is palpable to Mosley. For him "knowledge is
like that of someone standing at the top of the Tower of Babel and being
struck by the thought—what must things have been like before" (*Beyond
the Pale*). Like Bert, in *Imago Bird*, Mosley did not want to give up his
stammer which, like other psychosomatic afflictions, hangs on the cusp of

mystery, on the border of the knowable and the unknowable. "I thought—So this is where you get to, where there are no words left; where there is not light but pressure as if at the bottom of the ocean" (*Hopeful Monsters*).

3

Many of Mosley's obsessions surfaced in his early books. Even while evoking controlled spaces—Oxford in *Accident*, London and Africa in *Impossible Object*—there was still an interrogation going on. (His breakdown of male/female relations, of what Tolstoy called "the catastrophe of the bedroom," is devastating.) These books predate the *Catastrophe Practice* series by a decade or more. They contain elements of shock, moments when events suddenly surge ahead—similar to what happens in catastrophe theory. Mosley's forte is to show how intelligent and overly "civilized" people prey upon each other; his characters express base emotions that they deem unacceptable. It takes tragedy to get his characters thinking. The masterful *Impossible Object* is rife with—even riven by—tragedy and catastrophes, the electrocution of the narrator's son's girlfriend during a "game" in the basement, the drowning of a baby—without whom the man and woman might not have come to the sea (in a story called "The Sea") in the first place.

The car accident in *Accident* is the catastrophe that provokes philosopher Stephen Jervis's investigation and scrutiny. The novel defines a certain moment in the '60s. The restless Oxford don, weary at forty, in search of danger and inspiration through an infatuation with a beautiful, exotic student, was a man utterly divided, on "the edge of a cliff" without quite knowing it: he was comfortable in the past but drawn to the present. This is underscored not so much through the perennial theme of a middle-aged man obsessed with a young woman but in his corrosive envy—which he attempts to disguise with snarling contempt—of his colleague, fast-lane Charlie, a precursor of the celebrity academic, who hosts a television talk show.

4

Those who have seen *Accident*, the Losey/Pinter collaboration that is one of the best English movies of the '60s, will probably not associate it with Mosley's superb and innovative novel upon which it was based. The movie is pristine but glamorous, with Mosley's dialogic tension underscored by Harold Pinter's screenplay.

There is a scene in the movie in which the sound of bells accompanies the montage of gargoyles; it is as if the camera were lovingly saying good-bye to the ancient brick and bowers of England for the last time. Dirk Bogard and Jacqueline Sassard and Michael York glide over the leafy, sun-dappled river, while the light plays over them, each stricken with a divided passion.

Although this scene mirrors the stately tradition of lush, gorgeous writing that Mosley had mastered, before abandoning it, the passage in the novel, filtered through Stephen Jervis's psyche, is multilayered and pointillistic. Motifs recur, metamorphose, change in the changing light—the way perception is clarified over a short span of "real" time. Stephen Jervis is a man who, like several of Mosley's later heroes, realizes that he is trapped in his mind—in patterns of thinking that limit the world; that, while he is reaching for analogies and grappling with paradoxes, he is losing touch with where he is, with his body falling through time. I like Mosley because he is aware of what the novel can quarry from poetry. He works hard to pack a lot into his sentences, without overloading.

> I wish I had been able to understand all this; myself ungainly, on hands and knees, by Anna's legs. In the position of some old prisoner, Jew (difficult to say this); something archetypal in wrong clothes, boots, a mop and pail, a number. Looking up with that look we've grown accustomed to but even now do not quite believe; of terrible numbness and passivity. What was evil then? And outside me that seethingness of summer; the bright wood, blue velvet, water and trees (I say this again); the golden age, absolute, with couples and shining faces. Anna's dress was in minutely woven holes infinitely complex. . . . (*Accident*)

Jervis's attraction to Anna is catastrophic: he reaches for an extreme to counteract his own wild, chaotic desire, and he involves the reader completely in his negative reverie about being an outsider, a Holocaust victim, a "Jew." The shift back to the physical world—"And outside me that seethingness of summer"—after being so long inside the mind has terrific impact.

Pinter's screenplay objectifies this inner tension by having Stephen fall into the river and parade, his clothes dripping wet, across the common, while students and colleagues shake their heads in wonder. Though Mosley's association with Pinter may have been due to chance, the two men have similar ways of springing violence and menace or pure surprise after long, tense, buildups of pressure, as in the famous scene from *The Homecoming* when Ruth demonstrates to a room of men how a woman crosses her legs, or the scene in *Judith* when Judith pockets Oswald's cocaine to conceal it from the police on his behalf and ends up becoming addicted, or the moment in *Hopeful Monsters* when Max and his mother share a deliciously guilt-free incestuous moment (placing the family romance instantaneously on another plane). These seemingly discrete, isolated incidents, are analogous to electrons shifting orbits in particle physics.

5

Mosley locates the reader simultaneously in the world and in the mind. "But is not aesthetics to do with the fact that the structures of reality coincide with the structures of one's mind—" (*Hopeful Monsters*). There's an electric quickness to his writing—the precise novelistic equivalent of a Bach fugue for harpsichord—that gives his work an immediacy too often absent from the "novel of ideas." There is an immense difference between the "novel of ideas" and Mosley's novels about characters who have ideas. His compressed leaps are always emotionally impelled. The blows of consciousness are rendered in sentences that ask to be sounded out: stuttering jabs, feints, all dragging along this desperate desire to state everything at once. The violent shifts in syntax and discourse demand that the reader constantly look back. This multilevel thinking is accomplished frequently through a triple utterance: location of the speaker, statement risked, followed by a question (often with a dash instead of a question mark).

> I was sitting in the shade at the side of the square. I felt that I should look once more to see how that illumination was getting on in my head—
>
> If the universe is produced by an observer who asks this question—
>
> And has produced the observer who asks the question—
>
> Would not the required mutation be just the ability to live with this realisation?
>
> Quick! My pencil and paper—

Then— But before there can be the conditions in which such a muta-
tion can live, would there not have to be some sort of catastrophe? (*Hopeful
Monsters*)

What is even more remarkable is how this—and many other passages in
his work—replicates in miniature the vision of the Enlightenment, which,
in Michel Foucault's succinct account, reflects "the extent to which a
type of philosophical interrogation—one that simultaneously problema-
tizes man's relation to the present, man's historical mode of being, and the
constitution of the self as an autonomous subject." *Hopeful Monsters* makes
a forceful case that the energies of the Enlightenment are still potent,
still—potentially—useful instruments of change.

6

Scrutinizing several of the dominant scientific, philosophical, and psycho-
logical theories of this century, Mosley makes a bold attempt to forge a
synthesis. The very improbability of this enterprise works to his advan-
tage. There isn't an idea in *Hopeful Monsters* that isn't annihilated and then
reconciled. The plot unfolds through the stories and letters of the novel's
alternating narrators (who are difficult to tell apart): Eleanor Anders, first
encountered in *Imago Bird*, who is an anthropologist/psychiatrist, and Max
Ackerman, introduced in *Catastrophe Practice*, who is a biologist/physicist.
All the important characters in the novel with whom Eleanor and Max
come into contact—Mosley's amiable skeletons—are intellectuals, whose
dialogues remain at the same high pitch even on the battlefield. When
Eleanor and Max are miraculously reunited, he can't wait to let her finish
springing him from jail before engaging her with his new theories about
"coincidence." (How could eros not accompany a recognition scene in
which a woman unlocks a man's handcuffs?)

The book begins with Eleanor's account of the days surrounding the
"1914–1918 war": the buildup of antisemitic feeling in Germany; her
mother's involvement with Rosa Luxemburg (and vivid recreation of the
latter's grisly death); the public attack on Einstein's Jewish physics, "the
Theory of Relativity being contrary to the German Spirit." The brief close-
ups of these and other "real people" portrayed in the novel touch the nerve
of their ideas during those years. Mosley's quick takes vary from primerlike

summaries to elegant arguments to passionate pleas—as in Max's response to Einstein's refutation of Heisenberg and Neils Bohr: "Einstein may be right: it is not bearable that reality should be no more than a function of the experimental condition!"

7

Hopeful Monsters is almost documentary in its recounting of the *Wander-vogel* years between the wars; his characters wander around Berlin and the Black Forest; they dance naked before the light of campfires. Then history darkens: Kristallnacht, mounds of corpses on the battlefields of the Spanish civil war; then the creative/destructive axis of Los Alamos, where Max, working on the Manhattan Project, struggles to beat the Germans in the race to invent the atom bomb, "discovering what might be a suitable moderator for the irradiation of uranium so that a nucleus might split and produce further neutrons."

The cast of the *Catastrophe Practice* series turns up at the end of *Hopeful Monsters* to visit Max on his "*so-called* deathbed" (my emphasis). The book ends with Eleanor, the last to arrive in the ritual procession, asserting a kind of transcendent vision—like a random jump of particles—in the form of a question.

> [Max] said "I can't die!" Eleanor said "Why not?" Max said "Because I'm too happy!" Eleanor put an arm round him and held him. They stayed embraced. They were like one of those everlastingly happy couples on an Etruscan tomb. . . . Max said "For God's sake, something sometime has to die!" Eleanor said "I think it is the cancer that is dying."

9

Hopeful Monsters derives its title from two lowland salamanders, whose flickering tongues "move in jumps" like "the jumps of those particles that are on one level and then instantaneously they are on another." As a boy, Max became interested in the case of Dr. Kammerer, the Viennese biologist who had been accused of falsifying the results of his experiment with midwife toads (by putting ink markings on their pads to make it appear that they had inherited acquired characteristics). Max designs his own experiment; he wants to find out what would happen if he changed the environment (placing two lowland salamanders in a paradisal aquaterrarium to imitate an Alpine setting) "not to show the possibility of the inheritance of acquired characteristics—God forbid!—but to see whether from a setting that was aesthetic something new and beautiful might grow—something like a visitor from the future." Max's mother asks him, "What are hopeful monsters?"

> "They are things born perhaps slightly before their time; when it's not known if the environment is quite ready for them."
> She said "So you have made an environment that might be ready for them!"
> I said "Yes."
> She put her arms round me and hugged me. She said "You are my hopeful monster!"
> I thought I might say—But hopeful monsters, don't you know, nearly always die young.

Max is convinced that his experiment (and Kammerer's earlier experiment with salamanders) succeeded not because of the aesthetic environment he created for the salamanders but by virtue of his love for them. "Kammerer had perhaps loved his salamanders: but what was love?" Love is the part of the experiment that can't be measured. The best Max can do is "provide at least [his] salamanders with some setting in which love could operate?" It is also the mysterious force that keeps Eleanor and Max on parallel lines, gives them their thread through the maze, rescues them from impending doom. "Love is at the heart of things," Mosley wrote a quarter of a century ago in the "Suicide" section of *Impossible Object*, "like the particles that jump without reason or location." If Mosley-in-love sounds a little too easy—an upscale twist on the wisdom Pound came to in the *Cantos* with his refrain, "What thou lovest well remains"—it should remind us that his intent all along has been to enchant.

10

The morphology of Mosley's novels grows out of his thinking about interconnectedness: his philosophical concerns gain pressure and intensity by being filtered through his psychologically tormented characters. I love his portrayal of the young Max when he comes up against the wall of his

parents' recalcitrance (which mirrors their estrangement), their unwilling-
ness—in spite of their intelligence and accomplishments—to experiment
or to entertain the possibility that there might be some connection between his father's "discipline" of biology and his mother's study of psycho-
analysis.

> I said "But how much does all this tie up with what my father is doing in
> biology?"
> She said "Good heavens, in no way at all, as far as I know." She looked
> disappointed.
> I said "But shouldn't it?"
> She said "Why?"
> I said "Aren't they both to do with the things that go on between parents
> and children?"
> She said "I hadn't thought of that."
> I thought—But why haven't you thought of that?

Mosley shrewdly establishes Max's passionate curiosity, his bouyant response to frustration—("One can put oneself in the way of the experimental condition")—by way of contrast to his parents, without diminishing
what he owes them.

His narrators—bloodhounds where meaning is concerned—never tire of
reaching for parallels in history or science to get a grasp of what is really
happening within the "inner surface" of the visual plane. In one arresting
passage, children on a mound are first historicized; they

> are like Napoleon and his marshals surveying a battlefield: they watched sol-
> diers and cannon balls bounce and leap, flopping down like dead fishes. . . .
> —Or these children are rolling their tyres down the inner surface of the
> four-dimensional continuum of the universe to see what, at the end, will be
> the effects of light, of gravity.

Mosley is wonderfully tenacious in the way he interweaves the physical,
physics, and the metaphysical.

> I had sat down on my haversack at the edge of the wasteland at some dis-
> tance from the hill. I thought—I will stay here and observe not only the
> customs of this strange tribe but myself observing—
> —Out of the confusion of images, might something of myself get through?

There are probably too many references in the book to the effect of the observer on the observed. But Mosley uses this as a springboard into a moral dimension: he knows he is culpable and must make himself capable. Thought as action, action as event.

> It is a fact that this is a universe that has produced consciousness. But do we not also say, we physicists, that it is consciousness that in some way produces the universe: I mean produces what we see of the universe—this or that—and of what else indeed can we say is the universe? I mean—If what happens is in fact ordered by what we observe—by our act of observation—then of course the universe has evolved conscious beings that can observe, or how can it be what it is? What it is is the result of consciousness.

Hopeful Monsters has the tenor of a book that is addressed to the future. Mosley is willing to risk the unapologetically "hopeful," optimistic proposition that history, having made the wrong use of the right ideas, can still recover and repair itself. Questions themselves can change the molecular constituency of the particles around them so that eventually a catastrophe will occur and alter the language of our limits. Because thinking for him is a form of praxis, and he envisions consciousness as an environment capable of favoring mutations, Nicholas Mosley turns a book that might have been—with its fierce chronicle of deaths and destructions—"an illumination about terror" into one that redeems the time and becomes, against long odds, "an illumination about the nature of change?"

"A Non-Figurative, Perceptual Realist with Existential Overtones"

1

Jake Berthot has the rare and salutary ability to create problems for himself that are at once immensely difficult yet ultimately freeing in the way they complement his temperament—which is profoundly, as Stevens says of the mind, "never satisfied, never." I don't mean this at all in the tautological sense in which every artist is said to "fail" because the completed, or rather the abandoned, work always falls short of its status as pure possibility within the realm of conception; nor do I mean that he is gridlocked in competition with the painters he reveres and dialogues with. It's easy to imagine his "conversations" with Milton Resnick or Mark Rothko concerning the question of "how to take a given shape and respond to what that void seemed to present."

2

As a high school student in rural Pennsylvania, Berthot happened on an exhibition of the Abstract Expressionists at nearby Pennsylvania State University and saw the first paintings that set him on his way. Pollock stood out. "The paintings were like road maps, I can see now, and I felt, I guess, that I could travel that way with paint." It is a commonplace among abstract painters to single out Cézanne as their progenitor, but Berthot adds a neat twist to that formula when he singles out the Frankensteinian side of the master's attempt to "turn paint into skin." Berthot has a horror of his work being seen in terms of something else. He believes the way to make something real is "in the paint, the paint itself becoming."

3

In the spring of 1978 I had a long time to look at *Pennsylvania Road Trip* at the Whitney Museum because I was waiting for a friend, who was usually late, and I chose to meditate on the painting instead of fretting over my friend's irritating, if predictable, behavior. The canvas was receptive.

.   .   .

(And maybe I was drawn to *Pennsylvania Road Trip* because I was about to drive cross-country, and because it predicted that only after ten or twelve thousand miles of summer driving, when I reached Pennsylvania for a second time (heading east), would my mind—hurled from the chromatic West into the green of the East—lapse into reverie, navigate by automatic pilot . . . , and would I make the mistake of gauging my speed by the car in front of me to attract the highway police for the first time during that two-month drivathon?)

4

I saw the painting in 1978, but it was painted in 1969, when the war in Vietnam was at its height. Perhaps this accounts for Berthot's instinctive adoption of an unlovely army green with some red mixed in to render, or not render, the bower world of rural Pennsylvania? Since Berthot, in his wonderfully illegible/legible "writing" in his ink and gesso skull series, reproduces some equally ambiguous sentences by Adorno, it is not far-fetched to imagine that he was familiar with Brecht's chastening lines, where he suggests that in times like these a conversation about trees may almost be a crime.

5

(Since it had been fifteen years since I had spent those twenty minutes standing in front of *Pennsylvania Road Trip*, I wanted to see it again. While "owned" by the Whitney Museum, it lives in semiretirement—or sequestration—on a rack with other heavy, large, unwieldly paintings. It would take three men to take it down for me to view. I could help, I offered, but the curator said she couldn't let me do that. It was written that any painting owned by the museum had to be lifted out of its preservatory by museum employees. And she couldn't ask three employees to give an hour each of their time at the same time while they took it down and waited while I looked at it (since I wouldn't be there long enough to give them time to do anything else of substance so that they could reenfranchise it). I felt embarrassed at the idea that so much labor would have to be expended for something that was not absolutely necessary. I decided to think of it as another layer of the painting's exfoliating relationship with absence—as if it could ripen more the less it was looked at—for now.)

. . .

I remember that I had never seen the color of waiting, the variable army olive green, better explored than in this painting. But to get this color that is in some ways no color at all, the attractive plainness and subtlety of its ambiguity—this waiting that has so much to do with everything—Berthot had to find a way to paint time. And time out of time. The texture of time. Duration.

. . .

But time is not finite, like a canvas, and Berthot must have felt susceptible to what he calls "the unraveling that can go on forever." It was painted at a moment when people were excited, as they read the existentialists, about the idea of waiting as a metaphysical construct. And while it caused him to hesitate, to wait, this awareness gave Berthot a subject that is as fresh and challenging for a painter now as figuration and perspective were to the Old Masters: time. And time, in painting, is inextricable from deep space.

6

The noncolor of *Pennsylvania Road Trip* incites the viewer to respond actively; the documentary title increases the work's freedom from figuration. As I waited for my friend that day at the Whitney, I produced "Pennsylvania Road Trip," an experiment in syllabics (I had been thinking a lot about W. H. Auden at the time), for which I make no claims other than its appropriateness in this context.

> *Pennsylvania Road Trip*
>
> The hours, you could say, were endless,
> like the landscape, brown, unvarying,

not even the least midden to take
your mind off whatever pain provoked
through pain stripped of its accoutrements,

nothing either ahead or behind,
no square-bearded men in carriages
swishing and swishing like streetsweepers,
crow-gouged tomatoes, silent windmills,
just rectangular darkness, the end

turning back on the beginning, no
harvesters groaning to the edge where
tomorrow they'll mow the cornfield, more
distance, less sky, no chance to vary
the time until you cross the state line.

I wanted to do something really dry, powerful, yet resistant, something
that would, in saying what was not there, provoke—a recognition. Nine-
syllable lines (which end the incantatory power of the tetrameter and break
the flow of the pentameter) seemed like it had the right blend of freedom
and confinement; they caused a kind of hitch that reminded me of the notch
at the edges of the painting. The breaking of the grid.

In *Pennsylvania Road Trip* the flatness of landscape provides an eerie mirror
of the shape he was trying to paint, the rectangle. Through the stillness, the
emptying out, the spiritual vacancy of the painting, there's a murkiness,
a muddiness, that leans toward renewal. Since I don't construe this nega-
tivity negatively, I was happy to read an interview with the artist in which
he speaks of his later work as being "like a derailment," lacking the dreamy
flow of such early works as *Pennsylvania Road Trip* and such companion
pieces as *Green 2 Green* and *Lovella's Thing*.

Regardless of this self-assessment, Berthot has been willing, in an age
of hurry, to let himself develop—"Progresse" as John Donne inveighed
the "soule" to do—organically. Berthot has chosen a difficult and ardu-
ous "road trip." He has worked his way gradually toward a full palette,
building, *evolving*, color out of tone, without amputating himself from the
resources of tradition. I have no way of proving that Berthot's development has been so unforced, but it is not far from these vacant landscapes to

the densely populated skull drawings he was executing during the period I was looking at his painting at the Whitney.

7

If the peculiar and haunting absence of *Pennsylvania Road Trip* was Berthot's farewell to implications of the road laid down by Rothko and Resnick, his masterful skull series, in spite of its apparent (that is, very literally superficial) bleakness, paved the way toward a breakthrough.

· · ·

The best word I can find to locate the skull series is trialogical. While recalling Da Vinci's sepia anatomical drawings as much as any modern work with existential overtones, the skulls appear simultaneously to hover above a chiaroscuro background and interact with the painter's cursive script. Even without taking into account what the words say, the written signs are as oblique as the skulls themselves. Once again, without forcing his hand, Berthot landed on a composite image that provokes an unending conversation within its borders.

· · ·

There is nothing accidental about Jake Berthot's turn toward the skull for renewal. He is *obsessed* with origin, first things. His decision to draw skulls is also fortuitous because it allows him to return to the roots of drawing itself and the site where thought originates.

(For years he has been drawing in the margins of René Char's *The Leaves of Hypnos*—and it was in this war-journal-poem-in-prose that Char made his break with the destructions of the surrealists and solidified his pact with the pre-Socratics. Why is this significant? Because Char looked to a pre-Socratic vision to guide him through the seductive and alluring distractions of a "crenellated present" in which everything that had once been "of value" was now broken—torn shrieking from original light.)

What can be seductive in the eternal nothing is that the finest day is indifferently this one or any other like it.

(Let's cut this branch. No swarm will come to hang upon it.)

49

Answer "absent" yourself, or else you risk not being understood.

151

The morning silence. The apprehension of colors. The *chance* of the sparrow-
hawk.

152

(Translated by Cid Corman)

In a flash of intuitive rightness, whose implications, whose twist of logic
I doubt he could have foreseen or even intimated at the time, Berthot
let his skulls lead him, once he returned—violently—to color within several years time, toward the ovals and lozenges which provided him with
a probe, an entrance into painting's haunted, internal space. A space that
goes on forever. When you lose yourself in these woods, you do not hope
to be found.

William Arrowsmith in Heaven: A Sketch

> In this they [Agave and Cadmus] declare their humanity and a moral dignity which heaven, lacking those limits which make men suffer *into* dignity and compassion, can never understand or equal. This is their moral victory, the only victory the doomed can claim over the necessities which make them suffer. But it is a great victory; for by accepting their necessities in anguish, they claim the uniquely human skill of *sophia*, the acceptance of necessity and doom which teaches compassion.
>
> —William Arrowsmith, Introduction to *Bacchae*

*F*rom a letter to a friend:

I must confess Bill's death has disoriented me. It's as if a layer of skin has been removed.

.   .   .

The other day I asked my little boy why he was being so quiet. He said he was talking to his grandfather in heaven. I thought I should try to contact Bill there.

"How are things up there, old friend?"

"Lousy. There's no change in the weather. Everything's cut and dried, like a film by the dreadful Taviani brothers."

.   .   .

"Heroism ends in loneliness and death." W. A.*

*The quotes marked W. A. are taken from a variety of Bill's writings, mainly "Turbulence in the Humanities."

. . .

"Is there anything you can do to improve your condition?"

"I talked one of the precepts into having an Antonioni festival, but the prints were terrible—I could hardly hear for the crackling—and they couldn't get the original uncut *Profession: Reporter* with its earthly vision of heavenly transcendence."

"Did you get to see *Among Women Only* again?"

"You're thinking of the Pavese novel, *Tra Donna Sole*. Antonioni's adaptation is called *Le Amiche, The Girl Friends*. I forgot to mention that the idiot who ordered the films was confused about the Italian title, *Le Amiche*, and so we got some American film called *The Women*."

"That's hilarious. Especially since Cukor was known as the 'director of women.'"

"I guess it is. [Laughs. Coughs. Mutters.] These goddam allergies. They're killing me . . . no pun intended."

"Even there? I thought clear sinuses was one of the perks . . ."

"Your sins and weaknesses are magnified even in death, no matter where you end up. This is what everyone thinks the *Paradiso* is about—the absence of tension."

"The tension does lessen in the course of Dante's ascent."

"I suppose, but pain always accompanies vision."

"How are things otherwise?"

"The Nietzsche book hasn't had a single review. Twenty years of work down the tubes. . . ."

"Give it time. People will come to it."

"I suppose you're right."

"America isn't exactly in search of a tragic vision at the moment."

"I sent you a copy and you never wrote me a word about it."

"I'm sorry. I haven't been writing many letters lately, but that doesn't mean I didn't register the impact of the book. 'There is only one hope and one guarantee for the future of humanity: it consists in the *retention of the sense of the tragic*.'"

"OK. But people need to read these essays to clear out the misunderstandings surrounding Nietzsche's name—like the charge of antisemitism."

. . .

"If the hero had self-knowledge, he would never have become a hero."
W. A.

. . .

"It's frustrating having all these different projects so no one can see the line running through them. The classicists think I'm some quack. Do you know how many copies *The Occasions* sold in hardcover?"

"One thousand."

"Guess again."

"I see where you're heading. How many?"

"Two hundred fifty."

"I can't believe it."

"Neither can I."

. . .

I admit to being a little bit disingenuous in some of these exchanges. I couldn't bear to believe that things were quite this bad, that serious intellectual endeavor in America had come to this large an impasse.

Bill's Nietzsche book was endlessly delayed. And the eventual absence of response toward the project when it finally appeared, after semiology, structuralism, and deconstruction had all but taken over the seminar rooms, has some cruel ironies of which he may have been unaware. It so happens that *Unmodern Observations* (as *Considérations intempestives*) was the book that perhaps more than any other ignited the young Michel Foucault, who devoured it in the sun on the beach at Civitavecchia in August of 1953 and began his quest "sous le soleil de la grande recherche nietzschéene." It was one of Foucault's first great transgressions, because Nietzsche was still under suspicion after the Nazi appropriation of his man-hero.

Those students of structuralism and deconstruction in America who religiously sought out everything Foucault wrote that was in subtle and complicated ways fueled by these specific texts of Nietzsche's had in all likelihood never encountered "Schopenhauer as Educator" or "We Classicists." And while Foucault's biographer, James Miller, uses the Arrowsmith translation of Nietzsche's prose, he quarrels with his translation of the title, which Bill defended with characteristic vehemence.

> To render *Unzeitgemasse Betrachtungen* as *Unmodern Observations* may puzzle or vex those accustomed to *Untimely Meditations* or *Thoughts Out of Season*. But Nietzsche's intention was surely to alert his readers to the fact that he was writing not "unseasonably," but against the grain of the age, and the title must be translated with this in mind.
>
> . . . .
>
> *Unzeitgemasse* because they contain an explicit disavowal of the *Zeit*, the age, above all the present, now. They are not untimely, which means inopportune, nor unseasonable, nor out of season, which means little more than untimely.

Arrowsmith and Foucault: an unlikely combination. And yet we find Arrowsmith condoning the daimonic energies that set Foucault on his way. "Thus, his [Nietzsche's] philosophy is above all, like that of the pre-Socratics, a teaching, the unfolding thought of a self-mastering nature enacting its daimonic text."

.   .   .

And Arrowsmith as educator never tired of urging his students to become themselves. If this passage from Bill's translation of Nietzsche's scorching essay "Schopenhauer as Educator" did little to provide consolation, it did provide further instruction.

> For this is a kind of inquisitorial censorship which, according to Goethe, the Germans have brought to perfection: glacial silence. At least it was for this reason that most of the first edition of Schopenhauer's masterpiece had to be pulped. The looming danger that his great project might be doomed by indifference produced in Schopenhauer a terrible, almost uncontrollable anxiety; not one worthy supporter made an appearance. It is saddening to watch him searching for any sign of recognition; and his final piercing cry of triumph that he was actually being read (legor et legar) is somehow painfully moving. *It is precisely those traits in which the philosopher's dignity is absent that reveal the suffering man*, in anguish over his most precious possession." (my emphasis)

. . .

Ours was a friendship which *started* as a result of elective affinities. We shared a love for Antonioni, Eliot, Montale, Blackmur—though his was more exclusive, perhaps more religious. They could do no wrong. Our first meeting took place in the apartment he shared with his companion, Marianne Meyer, overlooking the Temple of Dendur at the Met. I was there to consult him about a project that concerned one of our mutual passions. I was nervous, but he made me even more nervous because of his nervousness. He ferociously devoured a bowl of pistachio nuts. The cracking seemed to mirror an inner tension.

On the one hand I remarked Bill's handsomeness, his bristling energy, his voice with its rich timbres—its uncanny resemblance to Richard Burton's voice; on the other I could not help but notice how thin-skinned he was—that after he voiced a strong opinion, he cast a sharp glance toward Marianne, like a little boy, seeking reassurance that he had not gone too far. At some point in our discussion it came out that I liked one of his dialogues on Eliot, and I was surprised and pleased that he seemed so surprised and pleased. (The current devaluation of Eliot was one of the crosses he had to bear—and rightly.)

He saw Antonioni as engaged in the same project as Eliot. The filmmaker had concluded a sketch: "Who is the third who always walks beside you?"
    "No one buys the idea that a filmmaker [Antonioni] can have an intricate pattern, an artistic design, and a consistent worldview that's evident in every frame."

. . .

Early in our relationship I sent Bill an essay I had written about the Swedish poet Tomas Tranströmer (in which I made an analogy between Tranströmer's dilemma and that of Locke's dissatisfaction with old codes in *The Passenger*). He fired off a letter of copious praise with one question/reservation: Did I know Swedish—and, assuming I didn't, how could I feel sure in my judgments? I responded that I never felt sure in my judgments.

How bracing it was to receive a letter from Bill, praising and excoriating.

He surprised me with a similarly intense response to an essay I had written, while still a student, about Heidegger and Trakl. I got him to concede that the concept of "aletheia" could be a lever, an active, search-provoking principle. (It was then that I got the story about his colleague's manic conversion to the idea of a single truth.)

.   .   .

"*Four Quartets* is the greatest long poem written in the twentieth century."

I always bridle at statements like this even if I agree with them.
"Maybe," I said, "but what about *The Duino Elegies, The Heights of Macchu Picchu, Baltics . . .*"
"In English then." He conceded that his generalization had overleapt.
"What about"—and now my imp of the perverse was set into motion and I could not resist—"*Briggflats.*"
"*You're going to tell me that* Briggflats is as great a poem as *Four Quartets?*"
"No. But I could make a case for it."
"I've never read *Briggflats.*"

I shouldn't have been surprised to hear this admission. Yet Bill's lack of interest in what he did not perceive as central to his concerns, his mission, did not diminish the meaning he could extract from his private pantheon of great artists and thinkers. His proclivity toward hero worship is another link in the chain of reasons why the Oxford series of Greek tragedies was the wrong project for him; but it seems of vastly more importance to me that he could articulate so well the qualities he saw in what he loved.

.   .   .

There came a time when I knew that when the phone rang at nine in the morning it would be Bill, calling to complain about New York, the noise, the fumes, the subway (which he took to NYU, where he was "allowed" to teach Marlowe and film and a course he devised on dialogue—"not classics"), but mainly, the absence of close association.

"What are you doing?"

"Settling down to work."

"Well, I've been up since five and I'm finished."

(Silence.)

"I'm desperate to finish this prose book."

"I envy you. I've got to write two introductions and then do something with this Eliot and Antonioni material."

(Pause.)

(Over a series of months Bill would send me copies of his essays on Antonioni and Eliot, which I would read and comment on. The essays on *La Notte*, *Red Desert*, *Blow-Up*, and *The Passenger* average about forty pages. Each one is liberally sprinkled with references to his touchstones: Plato, Leopardi, Nietzsche, Ruskin, and Eliot.)

"If it weren't for this goddam Greek series."

"Why don't you drop it?"

"I'm just so sick of . . ."

. . .

It's important to note that I only knew Bill in the last decade of his life, when he was, by several trustworthy accounts, a "changed man," having in fact a major change of heart after his first major heart bypass.

He had become more rigid in many ways but most noticeably with regard to his ideas about translation, deploring now the very moves he once made to make the classics come alive. "There are more important things than accuracy—there is life, for instance." His attack on the philologists only made sense in the culture he inhabited after the war, but once that culture ebbed away, as it began to do in the '60s, it made him almost complicit in its extinction. He began to hate the result of his own influence as it took shape in others, as if he'd unleashed a monster. It was easy to attack the philologists, but the seductive pluralism of postmodern theorists and translators gave him no target to aim at.

I think that deep down he believed that he was the only person who could translate Greek tragedy, Euripides especially, correctly. I once told him, half-joking (but only half!), that he should translate all of the plays by himself; and while he deemed this "impossible," I could tell by the hesitation in his voice that he liked the idea. (And why not? Murray did it. There was Wilbur's Molière. All of Euripides is shorter than the *Iliad*.) He began to hate the necessarily idiosyncratic twist each poet, who must work by ear to filter sense, gave to a text in the process of translating from one language into another—with its different set of signals.

People were always "going to call, going to get together, but they didn't." He said very pointedly (and poignantly) about an acquaintance who had disappointed him, "If you want to see someone, you see them." He was convinced that other translators of Montale were out to co-opt him. I didn't have answers to these things. (What would Bill have done *without* his enemies?)

What other people were resigned to thinking of as "the way things are" (Chamfort's "society" as the treacherous "Forest of Bondy") caused Bill to cry out with indignation. Out of respect for life.

. . .

It was anathema to Bill that a serious person should read anything for fun—relaxing one part of the mind to activate another. He was confounded by my love of hard-boiled detective stories ("you're a real Candide . . ."). When I told him that Brecht claimed to have read a "dime-novel every day," he quipped back, "I don't doubt it." When I told him I was reading *Little Drummer Girl*, he referred to John le Carré elegantly as "the espionage man." His unitary worldview allowed him to block out anything that wasn't central to his interests and obsessions, and so he was willing to risk the judgment that Antonioni was the greatest of filmmakers; but when I asked him what he thought about Godard, he said he'd "never seen a frog film."

He persisted in calling me during my working hours no matter how often I announced—too politely perhaps—that I was working. But for all my admiration of Bill, at those times I felt he was doing to me what Gabriel Ferzetti does to the young architect in the courtyard in *L'Aventurra* when he knocks over his inkwell and smears his drawing.

Once when he called to complain, I cut him short, "Bill, why don't you write an introduction and call the essays a book."

"It isn't finished."

"I've read over two hundred fifty pages—of tiny type."

"There are lots of themes I haven't touched. And films I haven't covered."

"Maybe it won't be the book to end all books—"

(There was a Causabon side to Bill.)

"It's not a matter of that—"

. . .

I didn't understand at this time that he did not want to get onto something else—that this was an entrenched strategy. After a brief show of resistance, which amounted to a statement of position, an acknowledgment of the boundaries of his recalcitrance, he would simply cease to respond to my entreaties.

"I'm sorry," he'd say with a note of finality and without any trace of apology—not that an apology was needed. I had the sense that he was no longer addressing me. His refusal was deeper. He would not, in this way, meet his maker. Bill lived inside his convictions, but his own experience had to be mediated through a mask. This was another source of his distemper. He lived his life under protest. He preferred to stay inside the shell, the persona, of the translator's masks and identify himself with another's vision.

Bill warred against those who would translate the words and miss the meaning. "Only philologists could have built their distinctive professional virtue—'objective' accuracy—into a theory of translation." I was struck by his severe appraisal of a recent much-needed translation of Leopardi's *Moral Essays* on the grounds that the translator followed the original in

linear fashion, instead of recasting it, transposing sentences and even para-
graphs when necessary, as Bill did in his *Satyricon*—having had the good
sense to learn from his friend Saul Bellow's opening-of-the-throttle prose
in *The Adventures of Augie March*.

·   ·   ·

What were his standards of criticism and scholarship? I knew of no books
that did what he proposed. Blackmur, in his detail-oriented essays, with
his desire to let the radiant particular stand for the whole—blasting Hart
Crane wrongly for imprecision in his line "peonies with pony manes" and
elevating Eliot for "The fog is in the fir trees"—is the closest approxi-
mation I can think of. Auerbach and Bakhtin, to name two of the most
synthetic critical minds this century has produced, in books on Dante and
Dostoyevsky, do not take you through each line of a poem or chapter of
a book; they focus on the details they need to underscore the points they
want to make. Bill made it a point to radiate outward. There was a madness
in his method.

Bill was attempting a synthesis through scattered projects that would
comment on each other, "advancing, not retreating," as he wrote apropos
of the *Bacchae*, "steadily into deeper chaos and larger order, coming finally
to rest only god knows where—which is to say, where it matters." And
those projects he did complete were also in rebellion against totalization.
(Why do I have to write about those I love so harshly?)

·   ·   ·

Bill invited criticism of his translations and nearly always incorporated sug-
gestions. Only once did he "get his back up" with regard to several lines in
the famous (in part because Montale wrote a short essay about it, defend-
ing himself from the charge of symbolism) "two jackals on a leash" section
of the "Motets." Bill insisted on calling the footman in gold braid ("un
servo gallanato trascinava") who drags the jackals a "flunkey." I thought
this made Montale appear more scornful and contemptuous than he was,
given his compassionate reminiscence of the old man as "dry and proud,"
with the voice of a "true uneducated Southerner." "Lackey," even though
another translator had used it (and Maurice English had called him matter-
of-factly "a liveried servant"), also seemed more colloquial and closer to

the sense of the original. Bill was unusually tenacious about this particular word choice, and we remained at loggerheads.

. . .

There is endless dialogue on what constitutes translation and what constitutes adaptation. A translator sees himself or herself as being faithful to the spirit of the original; and however far Bill strayed from the letter, or the original order of words, he tried, like a method actor, to imagine himself in the role of the writer were he writing in English. This is a formidable act of imagination. He became Petronius, Pavese, and Montale. They had the experience, they had imagined the scene for him, and he had the resources of the English language—language whose elasticity is often not plied by translators, who complain, instead, about the paucity of rhymes. (In a telling early review of Robert Lowell's *Lord Weary's Castle*, Bill telegraphs his own predilection for the hard-hitting Anglo-Saxon—and compound words.)

. . .

Edmond Jabès says, "One needs only a few markers to recognize a path," and William Arrowsmith did not have to read widely in contemporary American poetry to recognize that it was becoming increasingly swallowed up in its own lyrical "I"—which, gravitating toward humorless melodrama, had removed the possibility of a tragic voice. And so he intuitively gravitated toward Pavese and Montale as a corrective. Yes, there is a world elsewhere, but there is also a world *out there*.

It is another lesson Bill had drawn from the Greeks (and would draw him toward cinema): the necessity of action. And where modernity was concerned, the possibility of revelatory realism in which lyric and narrative are married: "To moderns this notion of character as expressive destiny is very strange, very Greek, indeed; even stranger is the idea, central to Pavese's work, that rhythm and meter are the temporal movement by which, *narrated*, this destiny is revealed." How far this is from trivial discussions of "technique"! Where any narrative is concerned, it is always a question of how to begin; and if you begin with action, other people, something happening, the poem has a chance of finding its way.

Anything can happen in the murk of the tavern.

—Cesare Pavese, "The Widow's Son"
(translated by W.A.)

And after that "anything," anything is possible. But, being human, we are most likely to find ourselves exhausted in our strivings toward the infinite.

The dead man is sprawled face down and doesn't see the stars;
his hair is stuck to the pavement. The night is colder.
The living go back home, still shivering.
It's hard to follow them all, scattering as they do.
One goes up a staircase, another down to a basement.

—Cesare Pavese, "Revolt"
(translated by W. A.)

It is not a question of whether this or that "version" of Pavese or Montale is the best poem in English among the other competing, yet complementary versions: the point is that Bill had a vision of Montale's ouevre; his translations amount to a vision of life. Anyone who imagines that this is an exaggerated claim should read and reread his introductions, notes, and commentaries, which lay the groundwork of a poetics. Bill believed that "his" poets were always recapitulating eternal themes and always intentionally recalling the masters. He was fanatical about this.

The poet does not "remember" time in the ordinary sense of "remember"; he sees things with awe—things revealed as if for the first time—and he thereby *becomes* memory itself, with the power to reveal the timeless "now" forever "waiting," immanent in the time of "things." By narrating "before" and "after," the poet narrates the experience of transience punctuated by "eternal moments"—moments when men become *memory* themselves by leaving time and living in a dimension of immortal clarity and meaning. And meter is the measure of mortal time and transience. By narrating it as it is lived—in the time of "things," illuminated by timeless, mythical meaning— the poet names a reality which physically and temporally corresponds to the tragic tension (brutal and divine) of human life.

.   .   .

Action is also active, or effective (*wirliche* is Nietzsche's word) history. It is the passing on not of knowledge but of the way toward knowledge—and the embodiment of it in living. This sense of living history is consummately portrayed in a scene Bill loved in *Philoctetes* when the agonized, uncompromising hero allows Neoptolemus to "touch" his bow. We hold our breath in those moments in which the bow is suspended between the two men.

. . .

Bill's translations were crucially his writings, his composite of voices. His translations mirrored precisely his central human concerns. There was fire in his versions of *Hecuba*, *The Birds*, *The Satyricon*, *Dialogues with Leuco*, and *Hard Labor*—a book that had terrific impact on American poetry through the poets on whom its influence ran deep. (He hadn't yet embarked on Montale.) We didn't know his prose—except for the newly appearing Eliot excerpts. This was a totally serious man, appealingly violent in his loves and hates, who could live simultaneously in the past and the present, to whom life was not some diminished thing. A humanist in a time when the very word had become suspect. Part sage, part gadfly. We cared that he cared! (I don't think he registered the esteem in which he was held by poets, fixating instead on his sense of being persona non grata with classicists.) He had more in common emotionally with our generation than his own.

. . .

There were those of us, who came of age in the late sixties and early seventies, who thought it was a good day when we uncovered an issue of *Delos* or *Arion* (which Bill founded and edited) in a used-book store. We relished the thrill of reading the kind of scrupulous, meticulous essay that could be encountered there, like Clarence Brown's modestly provisional version of Mandelstam's "Octets" along with a commentary on how the poem worked in Russian.

. . .

"All order worth having, Sophocles says, is born of the effort of turbulent men—men who do not know themselves—to surpass their limits and break down the barriers between man and god. They do this always to their own anguish, and they are seldom loved for what they do, until they are dead. This is because the hero is always an embodiment of turbulence, and therefore always threatens the order of complacement, self-knowing men." W. A.

.   .   .

I know no one who was more sensitive—and accurate—about the ways in which "the best minds of [his] generation" were ruined. He was critical of a respected colleague whose uncritical embrace of Heidegger's "aletheia" (his word to unlock the myth inside history, the "unconcealedness of beings" which is buried but recoverable) caused him to convert to this rather convenient notion.

.   .   .

Bill had a unitary vision of the world insofar as he perceived an order in the nodal points of thinking that passed from Plato (*ti allo*) to the concept of *arête*, to Leopardi's *noia* and its resurgence in Eliot's "nothing," to Montale's emphasis on *"what we are not"*—an absence at the heart of things that is a spiritual longing for "something else." His longing for transcendence fired his turbulence.

.   .   .

". . . man's most desperate bravery—trying to be moral in a world which offers almost no evidence of morality or meaning." W. A.

.   .   .

He was cogent in his rejection of rejection. I can think of no better illustration of Bill's general attitude than this interchange in *Coriolanus*.

> *Brutus:*
> There's no more to be said, but he is banish'd,

As enemy to the people and his country:
It shall be so.

Plebeians:
It shall be so, it shall be so.
Coriolanus:

                    . . . *I banish you.*
And here remain with your uncertainty!
Let every feeble rumor shake your hearts! . . .

                    (act 3, sc 3; my emphasis)

Coriolanus concludes his speech with a dazzling imaginative leap beyond the limits of his own circumstance:

                    There is a world elsewhere.

                    .   .   .

Was William Arrowsmith's behavior as volatile as it was because forces larger than he were crying out for him to act? It was as if the gods had decreed, as they say in film noir, that he should take the fall. To suffer—without surcease—like Philoctetes. To use his lively, fertile mind to do battle with retrograde, invidious forces. Invisible enemies. Too easily lured by battle, his own projects often suffered.

I am not a Jungian, but I do have the sense that something like a collective mind signals our attention to one thing and not another at that precise moment in time, in history. (For example, the lure of the church for such notable writers as Auden, Eliot, Greene, and Lowell "entre deux guerres" and afterward.)

                    Moths settle down on the pane:
                    small pale telegrams from the world.

                    —Tomas Tranströmer

Destiny is not always transparent, fated, or fixed. Artists are driven to do what they know needs to be done; they act for the race as a whole—driven to compensate for a lack that goes far beyond the deprivations in their personal histories. Beyond psychology.

.   .   .

All significant human activity exists in a realm that lies outside the boundaries of personal psychology.

.   .   .

> The riddle which man must solve, he can only solve in being, in being what he is and not something else, in the immutable. (Nietzsche, "Schopenhauer as Educator")

The collective mind, on its venal, thoughtless downhill course with regard to the classics and humanities, needed a spokesman. It nominated Bill to stand front and center, to write essays like "The Shame of the Graduate Schools"; it lured him away from tending his own garden. Another manifestation of this force is that this heretofore unspoken will (in the Schopenhauerian sense of the word) of the people "voted" for the "sexual revolution," *living* theater, and the like in the '60s once it had begun to recover from the trance-inducing (remember the body snatchers?) trauma of two world wars. Now its attention shifted to issues of ecology, abuse, the homeless, and so on . . .

.   .   .

This from a letter of Bill's to Stephen Berg printed in the memorial issue of *Arion*:

> The gods give men good and evil—*deal* men their fates. . . . If a man receives exceptional good fortune . . . it tells people that a "god" is with him; otherwise the exceptionality could not be explained. "God" is the sign of the prodigious, the strange, the uncanny; the lapse in the principle of sufficient reason. Anything prodigious or exceptional is "numinous." *But the reverse is, by the same logic, also true.* Exceptional *misfortune*, a terrible fate . . . is the sign of divine *notice*; otherwise it's not explicable. . . . The exceptionality of misfortune is the *sign* of gods at work.

.   .   .

Bill fought to keep the ground clear so that his contemporaries and "those who come after us" (Brecht) would have a better chance of being heard, understood. And so one reason he complained so bitterly was that he, William Arrowsmith, was unaware that he had not chosen all the permutations of this role, that forces outside his control had chosen him.

> The birds flutter to rest in my tree,
>   and I think I have heard them saying,
> "It is not that there are no other men
> But we like this fellow the best,
> But however we long to speak
> He can not know of our sorrow."

— Ezra Pound, "T'Ao Ch'ien's 'The Unmoving Cloud' "

.   .   .

In a culture in which people talk about "taking risks," at every instant Greek tragedy enforces the fact that life itself is always at risk. Count on anything at your own peril. Lull yourself into a feeling of security with regard to anything, and the catastrophe, when it comes, will be all the more horrible.

.   .   .

Live dangerously, Nietzsche exhorted. Bill had no choice: he was like a walking id, steaming and frothing, boiling over continually. He was childish. And yet part of what attracted people to him was that he was so much his uncensored self, "for these natures hate the necessity of pretense worse than death; and this continuous bitterness makes them volcanic and menacing. . . . They emerged from their caves with a ferocious look; their words are explosions, and they can destroy themselves. Schopenhauer lived in this way, dangerously." In a footnote to his translation of this passage, Bill added that it is an "echo of Achilles' words to Odysseus at Iliad 9:312–13: 'Worse than the gates of hell I hate that man who hides one thing in his heart and says another.' " With Bill, you knew where things stood.

One of his favorite phrases was "Why don't you get your back up about it?" When people were in contact with Bill, they felt relieved: they weren't being asked to sheathe their claws. And as touchy as he was ("What's the matter? Is something wrong?"), he liked to be disagreed with and, to give another contradictory flip to his domineering personality, he let you say what you had to say.

.   .   .

Bill was a "Leonardo" in his inability to finish anything of his own for fear it would not reach perfection, putting off, at all costs, the final (built-in? inevitable?) failure of the finished work. Translation allowed him deeper access to himself than criticism. He wanted dialogue—with Plato, with Nietzsche, with the poets he translated, with his friends. He felt deeply betrayed by the Academy's willingness to embrace deconstruction and explode humanism. Avid for life, as Montale has it, he wasn't at heart a critic—rather an essayist/philosopher, a teacher, in the vein of Montaigne and Emerson.

.   .   .

(A talmudic saying throws all this in another light: "It is upon us to begin the work, it is not upon us to complete the work.")

.   .   .

Bill harnessed his critical prose to the newly traditional academic forms, where range is measured too often by the number of references. Yet his dialogues on Eliot's French poems are among the heroic acts of mind in literary criticism. Who else could match the breadth of learning and insight that he brought to every line of Eliot's? Probably not even Eliot. He felt discouraged that this immense labor did not create more of a stir when it appeared in journals. And it would have done little to salve this aging giant's festering wound to tell him that the kind of response he desired was at best reserved for books.

But of course his paranoia was almost always in part justified. The prose he labored to translate in his later years, such as Nietzsche (even though begun many years before) and Antonioni's *That Bowling Alley on the Tiber*, received scant mention in the press, the latter because the director was stupidly out of fashion. (I didn't understand why Bill was willing to spend a whole day on the phone to get tickets at the last minute for a showing of Antonioni's *Identification of a Woman* at the 1981 New York Film Festival, because who would have guessed at the time that it would never have a theatrical opening in America?) When he shared the podium with Hugh Kenner and Christopher Ricks for a symposium on Eliot one evening at Columbia, the audience would be versed in their work, but how would they have come to know Arrowsmith's position . . . ? There was Bill among the major critics, and he had not published a book of his own prose. Another person who was best known for doing something quite remote from writing about modern literature might have been grateful for an opportunity to air his views in this company. It only occurred to me in the process of writing this that, *to my knowledge*, Bill, because he was so embroiled in the Academy's "who's in and who's out," did not register that the people who cared most deeply about literature and the humanities were immensely curious about what "Brigadier Arrowsmith" was hatching.

.   .   .

"Brigadier Arrowsmith." Carne-Ross hit the target with that. His body language, his speed and burliness (accentuated by his standard turtleneck and cowboy boots) as he moved through the throng of students, brought to mind the image of a general leading his troops.

.   .   .

There was nothing of the charlatan about Bill. He made no false claims to be saying something new. He complained that some classicists cast him as a popularizer, which he most definitely was not: he was an artist doing the job he knew needed to be done even if it meant that he had to sacrifice himself in the process.

.   .   .

His prose works are also documents that preserve in pristine form the connection between the ancient and the modern. Bill's trump card as a critic:

his knowledge of the classics, how they interact with the contemporary. His absolutely religious belief in tradition empowered him.

We think of "commentaries" as a dogged kind of scholarship, yet Bill was almost winged in the speed with which he vaulted the immeasurable distance between now and then. And he was clear in his motivation: that behind each of these focused creative acts, these—explosions—, there was very little actual difference between the classic and the contemporary because the terms of what it means to be human have changed so little over this mere two millennia that separate "us" from "them"; that literature is about what it is to be human; and that to be human is to be torn, rent, divided between the bestial and the divine. The classics are human-centered; they focus on how human beings reveal who they really are: their passions, their—*acts*. (Which is what led Goethe, in *Faust*, to venture that in the beginning was the act, and Wittgenstein to embrace that notion toward the end of his last work, *On Certainty*.) Bill was drawn to an action-centered literature where there is less separation between what people (albeit characters, lyrical voices) say and what they do.

.   .   .

In *The Storm and Other Things*, Montale shows *nature* disturbed as he enters into one of history's darkest moments. He insists that the voices issue from an inner dialogue which does not exclude politics but never obeys any mandates of fashion or places the topical above the elemental. Here neither the wind nor the flight of birds is innocent, or exists out of history.

In Montale, the allusions are subsumed into the body of the text; they have undergone a metamorphosis before they enter the line. There is no patchwork of quotations; the poems are direct, the obscurity more a result of what he has left out. Montale is a master of the fluid image that spreads and contracts out of a hard core through the tissue of the poem and comes to stand as an emblem.

> The ring-necked solferino doves
> have come to Sesto Calende for the first time

in human memory. So the newspapers
say. Peering out the window,
I haven't spotted one. A necklace of yours,
but of another shade, snagged a reed at the top,
and its beads crumbled. Only for me it flashed,
then fell in a pond. And that fiery
flight blinded me to the other.

—Eugenio Montale, "From the Train"

In his "Notes" Bill labored to unpack the layers of allusion woven into Montale's sinuous lines.

The mediating term . . . is the explicitly Dantesque word, *bufera*—at once the "storm" or better "tempest" of war, but also the terrible "storm of passion," the infernal wind that in Dante (Inf. v, 28 ff.) *whirls* and *batters* those stricken by carnal passion. The careful reader will need the text present to his mind throughout.

> *Io venni in loco* d'ogni luce moto,
>   *che* mugghia, *come fa mar per tempesta,*
>   *se da contrari venti e combattuto.*
>
> *La* bufera infernal, *che mai non resta,*
>   *mena gli spiriti con la sua rapina;*
>   voltando *e* percontendo *li molesta.*
>
> I came into a *place mute of all light,*
> which *bellows* like the sea in tempest,
> when it is combatted by warring winds.
>
> The *hellish storm,* which never rests,
> leads the spirits with its rapine;
> *whirling* and *battering,* it vexes them.

Out of this Dantesque passage and the hellish locale, M's governing terms are generated by allusion, expansion, transmutation, or opposition. Evil is everywhere associated with the Dantesque darkness—feverish sleep, lingering night, deepening gloom, the ominous gathering of groaning voices, shattered light. The world is perceived as a Dantesque ditch: fosse, mire, bog, slimy marsh, sewer, morass, even magma—"the great bog teeming with its human/tadpoles opens to the furrowing night." Acoustically, this human hell is cacophony: thunder, sistrums, cracking sounds, shattering crystal, tambourines, shots, the airplane roar of giant wing-casings buzzing. And, whirled by the great *bufera*, is the dance—fandango, jig, sardana, saraband—of dervish circularity, meaningless turning on itself. The human beings themselves are: the stillborn; the skeletons; the imploring hands of victims reaching up and out of the marsh; the shattered wings of what was once a tremulously flying thing, a fallen bird.

To read Bill's introductions and commentaries is to be directed toward the sources that matter because they contain, in the most refined, distilled form, crucial information about how to survive the necessary vicissitudes of a human life.

A classic is a record of what humanity knows about itself at a given moment in time.

But he never stopped addressing himself to the deaf, the enemy—stolid, crusty classicists who needed to be corrected—to blithe, carefree (and careless) contemporaries (he actually takes on Kael, Siskel, and Ebert with regard to their misreading of Kurosawa's *Kagemusha!*) who canonized and reviled works which they had not begun to understand. To misunderstand *Kagemusha* out of ignorance of clan lore (which could, Bill rightly insisted, be ascertained in an hour's scan of any standard history of Japan) or a failure to see what was really happening on the screen, was to perpetuate falsities. These falsities serve in turn to collectively create a lie that would in all likelihood be mistaken by many as the self-evident truth. It didn't bother him that people misunderstood, saw differently or didn't like what he liked, but their apathy incensed him: the notion that they just wanted to get a job done. Bill's antipathy to this culture of hurry, of technology progressing fast beyond the present human capacity to use it—and grow along with it—drew him to the master diagnostician of its symptoms: Michelangelo Antonioni.

Those who speak of Bill as a hero do so for a reason: they were privy to his labors on behalf of what he believed to be true.

. . .

There are two films I longed to see more than any others, *Le Amiche* and *La Nuit de Carrefours* (an early fog-drenched Renoir—with a missing reel—in which his brother Pierre plays Inspector Maigret). So when I noticed in a brochure sent out by the Museum of Modern Art that *The Girl Friends* was playing one evening (and only one), I called Bill in Boston to alert him. He and Marianne flew in. When he was happy, as he was that evening, he beamed.

His capacity for joy was immense. Frustration made him churlish.

. . .

Once, en route to Maine, Madelaine, Sam and I stopped to visit Bill over-night in Brookline and witnessed several other sides of this testy, ebullient man. He was a conscientious host. He followed Sam, who was fifteen months at the time, around without a trace of impatience as he rummaged through everything at floor level. Keenly attentive to the child's move-ments, he noted with pleasure that "he has to touch and smell everything, like an animal." But the shocking thing was not the extensive library or shelves of CDs but how well stocked his wine closet and kitchen cupboards were, loaded with specialty items—chestnut marrons, dried mushrooms, canned cuttlefish, three kinds of olive oil—a storehouse worthy of a gour-met fallout shelter. He announced he was cooking risotto. At one point he exclaimed, "I'm exhausted, I've been standing on my feet all day by the hot stove." Madelaine and I looked at each other: we both knew where we had heard the expression, the tone of voice, before: my mother.

. . .

"The story of the snakebite is not the story of how Philoctetes acquired his famous wound, but rather a symbolic account, in temporal sequence, of what Philoctetes *is*. He is the sort of man who invades a sacred shrine—who aspires to divinity—but who is always pulled down and back by his festering foot—his incurable animal nature. In short, he is Sophoclean man, torn and tormented by his double nature, half god and half brute, the aspiring animal." W. A.

. . .

In November of 1986 my father jumped from an eleventh-story terrace in Miami and landed head first in the parking lot. And while I did not feel responsible, I did have—to put it mildly—conflicting feelings. Around that time I was reading Charles Kingsley's children's version of the Theseus story to Sam. I was fascinated by Theseus' failure to carry out his pact with his father to take down the ship's black sail and hoist a white one in its place if his mission was successful.

Where were the secret texts about Theseus? Why hadn't psychologists seized on the permutations of this story? For starters, Theseus might not have known, or foreseen, the radical steps his father would take if he did not see a white sail. Maybe he was still high from his thrilling victory over the Minotaur and assumed his father had faith that he would triumph. And surely Aegeus *could* have waited for further evidence that his son was dead before he leapt into the sea. (How pitiful he looks standing feebly on the cliff's edge scanning the empty horizon in Federico Castellon's vivid illustrations.)

Thinking about the Greeks always made me think of Bill. We hadn't spoken for a while, and I used my new obsession as an excuse to call him up; yet when I asked him where I might find more about Theseus, he said, "Theseus! He's one of the least compelling mythic heroes. Why are you interested in him?"

I found it strange that he found it strange that I should be so curious about Theseus, given the circumstances of my father's death. It did no good to tell him this. He was genuinely baffled by the odd directions, the detours, other people took in their thought.

I told him what I knew of the story, the eerie way in which, to me, Aegeus's leap into the Aegean mirrored my father's, the question—one among many—of how the son is burdened by the father's ruin. Bill was combative but *listened*; and after his rather charming fit of pique (about which those who did not know him will have a hard time understanding that it had more to do with the larger question of the loutish Theseus than with me, or anyone) he would do whatever he could to help. And in this case surprised me by recommending a novel by Mary Renault—an erstwhile best-seller which occupies its niche in so many country inns. No, I explained, I was looking for a more authentic source. He railed, "Mark, you're talking about Theseus as if he were a real person." While this was by all means an affectionate sort of rant, his response confounded me further, given his passion with bringing the classics to life.

Two years after his death I came across this quotation from Plutarch, in "The Shame of the Graduate Schools" (reprinted in the memorial issue of *Arion*), strategically placed as an emblem of how "in the ancient world generation competed against generation and hero against hero."

> Theseus had long been secretly fired by the glorious valor of Heracles and made the greatest account of that hero, and was a most eager listener to those who told what manner of man he was. And it was quite obvious that Theseus felt what for many generations Themistocles felt, when he said he could not sleep for thinking of Miltiades' trophy. In the same way Theseus admired the arête of Heracles until his nightly dreams were all of the hero's achievements, and by day his ardor led him out and spurred him on in his purpose to do as much.

. . .

He *did not* complain when the book jacket of his translation of Montale's *The Occasions* advertised his forthcoming version of *Ossi de Sepia* as *Cuddlefish Bones* instead of *Cuttlefish Bones*. This earliest of Montale's books retains its freshness in Bill's version: he needed all of his resources—his syntactic knottiness, his skill at enjambment, his intuitive sense of what could be brought into living English—to make it work. *Cuttlefish Bones*, lush, rapturous, full-throated, yet almost hallucinatory in its exactitude, capturing the blaze of light bouncing between water and stone on the coast of Lerici—and the unmitigated gaze of childhood and youth—is also Montale's "Seascape with a Frieze of Girls."

. . .

Montale combines nihilism and vitalism, ennui and ecstasy. Images are emblems. The weather is the mirror of the soul. The monotony of clock time is redeemed "by what seems an occasional/burst of castanets."

Bill chose to translate Montale's first book after its successors, *The Storm and Other Things* and *The Occasions*. This makes sense because *Cuttlefish Bones* is a descent, even a regression, into a world of fresh sight, which always brings its accompanying dangers. Montale sets forth his early poetics decisively in lines that predict the fructive negations of Beckett and Celan:

> Don't ask me for words that might define
> our formless soul, publish it
> in letters of fire, and set it shining,
> lost crocus in a dusty field.
>
> Ah, that man so confidently striding,
> friend to others and himself, careless
> that the dog days' sun might stamp
> his shadow on a crumbling wall!
>
> Don't ask me for formulas to open worlds
> for you: all I have are gnarled syllables,
> branch-dry. All I can tell you now is this:
> what we are *not*, what we do *not* want.

In *Cuttlefish Bones*, Montale faithfully records the steps, the radiant particulars, that led him to a sense of rapture, and the book is written with an acute consciousness that chance mediates between the confluence of the personal and the public: he will never be this "wide-eyed" again, and history is darkening. *The Storm and Other Things* are coming.

· · ·

Cuttlefish Bones is an oratorio and an outcry, an assertion of plenitude in destitution—a fullness of being that presents the possibility of undiminished life rendered precisely at all times without recourse to the D'Annuzian rhetoric that begins with a poet's predisposition toward language and subject, rather than, as Dante asked for, a wringing out of the poetic *material*. In *Cuttlefish Bones*, language finds its way, gropes, twists, turns, as it struggles to embrace an imagined object.

this is the moment, so long awaited,
that frees you from your journey, link
in a chain, unmoving motion, ah, that too familiar
ecstasy, Arsenio, of inertia. . . .

Montale became more pledged to objectification in his later poems, so readers feel they can still hang their hat on the prose of fact. In "Arsenio" he opens up a form of objectification, similar to Eliot's but significantly different, whose ramifications still constitute a challenge to the imagination. This is how Montale put it in his "Imaginary Interview":

A new non-Parnassian way of immersing the reader in medias res, a total absorption of intentions in objective results. In this I was also driven by instinct, not by theory (I don't believe that Eliot's theory of the "objective correlative" existed in 1928 when my "Arsenio" was published in The Criterion.

.   .   .

Bill, who grew tensions, lived a dialectical life. He had no desire to dissolve contradictions or even try to cure his restlessness.

In the summer of 1985, when Bill was in Martha's Vineyard, I wrote him a letter from the Maine coast, evoking the effect of light on the pink and black micaed rocks, and how the multicolored stones would blaze as we walked over the shore trail speckled with chanterelles and delicate white pipestem flowers.

He wrote in response: "I turn my back to the window and work. For the night is long in which no man can work."

My Best Friend

This criminal is dangerous
The criminal under my own hat
—T Bone Burnett

PROLOGUE

*I*n the dream I'm back in the classroom across from the one boy I'd hoped never to see again. We're seated at opposite ends of the room. I can't tell, from the fixed gleam in his eye and constant smile, if he remembers me or is just reacting to my glance. What's happened to the others? They're not down in the nether pool area, where swimmers' strokes crease the water between taut-stretched ropes. This is where we would have gone to high school if we'd gone in a straight line in our district in Chicago, but James is the only one of my classmates who remained. Me, I only came back for a look, with hope of seeing the others, but my dream denies my wish. Still, James stayed out of jail, no small accomplishment for someone so volatile. He's the one who stayed outside the orbit of my affections, a boy whose cruelty seemed to have no root, who picked a fight because he felt like it that day, and punched so rapidly I could not see the fists that sent the blood spurting from my nose and reddened my ears, his hands too quick to interrupt with words. Are the others lost because I sought them?

I

"I seem to remember a lot of traffic in and out of our apartment at 5000 South Cornell."

"Why do you always have to repeat the addresses of the places in our past? I know it's not showing off because you do it no matter what the address signifies socially, monetarily . . ."

"That shows how much you know. Because if I know Mark, you've plunged right into the center of your story without setting the stage."

"It's not a story."

"Your father was right. You do hang on words. But now those who are familiar with Chicago will know exactly what the dynamics were in that neighborhood."

"And those who are not . . . ?"

". . . that our apartment was near Hyde Park, on the border of the mainly white well-to-do north side of Chicago and the mainly black neer-do-well south side."

(Pause.)

"Don't blow up! I couldn't resist the parallel. You can always substitute African-American neighborhoods of the south side. But, since you know—I mean you do remember that I fought for civil rights all my life—I was no racist, I will admit (since we've always been straight with each other) that I was thinking of the vagrant fathers in that black community whose absence contributed so much to the fate and suffering of your friends, like that Ulysses Washington."

"You remember Ulysses?"

"Remember him? Do you remember all the times I went to speak to the principal to get him to stop knocking you around?"

"I do remember one time . . ."

"There were many . . . I suppose you don't remember the afternoon, several years later in Kankakee, when I showed you the item in the *Chicago Tribune* that 'Ulysses Washington, aged sixteen, killed his grandmother because she wouldn't buy him a pair of black chino pants.'"

"Maybe."

"Not maybe."

"We have different kinds of memories."

"You only remember what you want to remember."

. . .

What remembers me?

2

It had to be on one of those auspicious days, days when you wished for some clouds, that the sun showed up in all its regalia, bouncing off every passing van or chrome hubcap, so that the rusty, pallid, chain-link fence blazed, igniting the gravel. It had to be amidst these cruel refracting reflections that Sidney made his way from the entrance at the chain-link fence toward the steps leading into the school itself, so that every kid in school could watch and see that he was connected to me: I, who had nowhere to hide, even as I tried to disappear, nowhere to hide from Ulysses, who didn't need a diagram to figure out that Sidney had come to talk to the principal on my behalf. I felt misunderstood: *I wasn't a snitch* but I was desperate—and outnumbered. Ulysses couldn't keep himself from attacking me; he loved to fight just as I hated to and he was older, faster, stronger than me. And so I felt driven to ask Sidney *to do something*. But not this. Not come to school as school was starting so that I could get into deeper shit by becoming known as a snitch.

. . .

At the moment Sidney put his foot on the steps of Kenwood Elementary, Ulysses flashed a radiant smile at me and I smiled back. His teeth gleamed. He approached me in such a friendly manner that my heart melted. And no threats. "That your Dad?" he asked, knowing it was, as if excited to see him. "Yeah." "He's got a cool hat. Where'd he get that hat?" "I dunno." It was his way of saying he knew I had to do it and he knew that it would not change our relationship in any essential way. How can I describe it? Because we were *friends*.

"You know what? I like you. You and me can work things out."

Ulysses put his arm around me. "You're my best friend." I tried to explain: *It's not really you he's come to complain about, just certain things you do that are not really you. Why do you do them?*

"Excuse me."

"Sure Mark, what's the matter?"

Mark!

"I forgot to tell my Dad something." And then I ran. Caught up with him just in time. "Look, I've been thinking. I don't think Ulysses's going to do it again. In fact, he's my best friend."

"No. I came here because you asked me, and I'm going to talk to the principal."

I stood in front of the opaque corrugated glass.

"They'll call me snitch. It'll make things worse."

"All right, but from now on you're on your own. Any more problems between you and Ulysses you'll have to work them out between yourselves."

That wasn't what I wanted to hear, but I wagered that if I came home really bruised and bloody he'd forget this ultimatum.

.   .   .

I was at a slight disadvantage physically. Ulysses was the toughest and most streetwise kid in our class. It's true that Ulysses would often pick a fight with me; it's also true that sometimes he'd prick me with a switchblade; but I knew that Ulysses would go no farther than drawing a little blood; I knew he wouldn't kill me (though in addition to the pain, I didn't like it when he got that far-off look on his face and he seemed to forget whose head he was knocking against the pavement). So I was angry when my parents outlawed him from our house and he had to climb up the fire escape and come in the back window in order to play. And Ulysses was never cruel while in our house. This was the heart of our relationship: it was a conspiracy. But in public Ulysses wanted the other kids to think this was not so and so would turn on his heels and start pummeling me at recess, before or after school, and after Ulysses, James would have a turn; James who crooned in his Sam Cooke voice as he punched, James who, though smoother on the outside, didn't have a secret warm spot in his heart like Ulysses.

.   .   .

Me and Ulysses were pals. Not best friends exactly but close to it. I had no idea at the time, when we both attended Kenwood Elementary School on the south side of Chicago, that he was eleven and I was only eight—I guess we were children, though it didn't feel like it then. And I doubt Ulysses knew the profound effect he had on me.

.   .   .

Ulysses was an orphan. He lived with his grandmother, who cleaned apartments, when she could get the work. Ulysses had sauce, personality. He led—seemingly without effort. Of course, this could have been due to his age. Fourth grade was to become Ulysses' impasse: he couldn't get over that wall, and it was time to knock it down.

.   .   .

I remember the expression on Mrs. Klein's face when I entered her classroom: delight, relief. At last—another refugee from the middle classes. If there were any other white boys in our class, I don't remember them. But there were, by some peculiar sleight of demographics, several girls: Karen, Karen, Karen, and Louisa.

There were a few quiet, unassuming kids in the class who never got into a fight. They didn't scramble for the ball at recess; they ate lunch quietly in the corner of the cafeteria. Though shy to the point of mortification, I forced myself to put up a good front and not reveal my vulnerabilities. But there was a wildness, a wilderness in me that drew me to Ulysses. I had to know Ulysses' world.

Mrs. Klein would often throw me a wide, inviting smile when I came back from recess, and I, smarting from my wounds, would smile back. It was amazing how little blood there was to show for the amount of pain endured. And there was never any question of my informing.

I didn't like this survival of the fistiest. I wanted to hug Karen, not smash James in the face. "C'mon, c'mon, white boy," he'd say, dancing lightly around me on the playground. "Whatsamatter, got no guts?" His jabs hurt more than blows: they wounded my self-esteem.

While I indulged myself in these escapades, Sidney hung his hat on the antlered rack of General Julius Klein's public relations firm, and my mother worked happily for an advertising saint with a name I could never get my mind to bend around, Dell Girlie.

.   .   .

My teachers loved me or hated me.

.   .   .

Ulysses had no parents, and I had three.

.   .   .

I was a boy. But I hated fighting, and contact sports. I wanted to protect my head. I adopted a warrior's pose, a camouflage of white T-shirts with the sleeves rolled up and blue jeans and motorcycle boots. I smoked cigarettes that were a cinch to pilfer, along with small change (a windfall fortune) from my mother's purse.

If it hadn't been for Ulysses, I might not have adopted my camouflage. If I hadn't met Ulysses, I might not have thought to move on from robbing pennies from the nun's poor box while she looked on with compassion for my weakness to my mother's bulging change purse, waiting there in her open handbag, nor learned how to quadruple my ten-cent allowance with very little effort or risk of being caught.

.   .   .

One day Ulysses knocked at the window on the fire escape, and all I could see was his body against the sky, not where his feet were planted. I opened the window and he hopped in. We were both gleeful at his daring. The nerve! The resources! The simple, elegant solution to his banishment!

Ulysses seemed utterly at home in my room with my toys. Electric trains would have made too much noise to play with, so we lined up toy soldiers, blew them away, and brought them back. Ulysses put a couple of howitzer bearers in a drawer and said, "You can't get those."

I raided the icebox and fruit bowl. Ulysses stuffed his pockets with apples and bananas and cookies. I could see he liked me better than he ever had and that this visit would alter our relationship forever.

.   .   .

"Wasn't that . . . Eugenies . . ?" my mother observed as he disappeared down the fire escape. "I mean isn't that the boy who's giving you such a hard time?"

"Yeah. But we're friends again now."

"Oh. That's good. I mean I guess that's good."

.   .   .

I am not exaggerating Ulysses' toughness. But he was a sprite, a Jiminy Cricket compared to the high school kids who waited for the grade-schoolers at the soda fountain after school. These were kids whose eyes couldn't focus anymore, who barely moved their lips when they uttered their threats and tapped the side pockets of their army fatigues to let you hear the sound of metal clanking. They bored themselves with their own demands. "Gimme your money kid and you can go."

I was angry and afraid, but what really threw me was the terror in the eyes of the guy who owned the candy store. He watched, from behind the counter, in his white smock, and I could hear him swallowing, gulping, dry-mouthed with fear. He was afraid to call the police for fear of further retaliations. This was real life, and *there was no one to help*. But I was damned if I wanted to hand over my meager allowance on a Monday afternoon before I'd had even a Coke or an egg cream. Ulysses was walking by. He came to the grimy window and rapped on the glass and waved. "Mark!"

Whenever he used my first name, I knew he was well disposed toward me. "Gotta go," I said, breaking free from the circle of negative magnetic energy the teenagers had installed around me. Ulysses broke the spell of fear, and as we broke into a run, I asked him if he knew what was happening in the store. "No, man, I saw you and I knocked on the window." Simple questions, simple answers.

Ulysses was so fearless he hadn't even noticed!

"Ulysses," I said. "I want us to be friends forever."
"You got it man, you got it."

.　.　.

Ulysses knocks on my window from the fire escape.
"Come out, man."
"But it's late, dark."
"That's all right, come on."
So Ulysses and I prowl the avenues and side streets and vacant lots. In the neighborhoods where we walk there is hardly another body on the street. There is nothing to be afraid of, really, in the late 1950s in Chicago; what I feel is a sense of awe at the vast windy spaces, the way the prairie keeps breaking through the vacant lots. This is a wilderness upon which concrete has been imposed.

.　.　.

I didn't think of the streets as dangerous, except around the school. I had no fear whatsoever of adults, strangers as potential kidnappers; I mean, anyone who fucked with us would have been crazy—we were armed and dangerous, though I had sworn to myself never to use more in self-defense than a roll of pennies clutched in my fist: I was afraid of repercussions.

Of course I knew that I was white and middle-class and that Ulysses was black and poor. But Ulysses seemed to know infinitely more of life than anyone else remotely my age. What I didn't know was how desperately Ulysses didn't want to go home.

3

I had two other black friends, Paul and Rex. Paul was my real best friend, but since our relationship was satisfying and without crucifying tensions, I have less to say about him than Ulysses. Paul was a sweet boy who managed to stay out of harm's way. Some of my happiest afternoons were spent with him trading comic books. We both came out winners.

But going over to his house was a real shock. Because it was dark. Darker than it was outside in the autumnal haze amid the repartee of reflections. We sat poring over comic books in the fading light that barely entered the opaque window of his dreary, gray, airless living room, a stage set with the scantiest of props. The floor was bare, the furniture droopy. I perched lightly on a jut of the collapsed yellowed sofa. His mother, a sourpuss with a broom, tensed her face when she looked at us playing while she busied herself. The absence of light in Paul's house weighed heavily on me.

This was why Paul was so rarely allowed to play after school: he had to do his homework by daylight. This saddened me. I thought *light* was a common property; I couldn't imagine being so poor as not to be able to afford a light bulb.

I returned home with a mission. My mother's cupboard bulged with light bulbs, and I knew she wouldn't miss the half-a-dozen I extracted on Paul's behalf. The bare living room wouldn't be exactly cheerful, but at least he would be able to read.

I wrote my father in New York to tell him about how much I was enjoying my new life in Chicago and to ask for money to buy light bulbs for Paul. I tore open his letter in the brisk November air, under the awning of our apartment house, and lit upon the phrase, "I'm happy to hear you have some negro friends." His reply crushed and angered me. Negro? How could he call my friends *negroes*? I felt demeaned by the word, having confused, or rather conflated, it with "nigger." I sensed a certain condescension in his tone: it set up an invisible (invincible?) barrier between myself and my friends.

Yet nothing in the letter said anything bad, and for all I know I overreacted and misread (in this case) the tone, and I must, in some form of communication to him, phone call or letter, have referred to Ulysses and Paul and Rex as something other than "white male caucasian."

If they're *negroes*, I wondered, what am I?

.   .   .

The next time I went over to Paul's house, the situation had not improved. I was stumped by this conundrum. They hadn't even put the bulbs in the sockets. More than a decade passed before I realized (because I had often meditated on this event) that the problem lay not in their lack of bulbs but in their inability to pay the electric bill.

It bothered me that Paul did not complain, that he did not see it as his right to complain. (But how to separate that from the natural sweetness of his temperament?)

.   .   .

Being an only child, my friends became my family. I loved my friends, and I lived out of the house as much as was possible. I longed to be part of a community, and I didn't see any problem in creating one.

Black kids had another fashion in which I found a certain novelty. Many came to class with stockings on their heads. Everyone acted as if this was perfectly natural. I asked Sidney about this phenomenon. "They have ringworm," he said, "and it's very contagious. It comes from living in squalid, dirty places . . ." And once more the association of dark skin, bad light, and squalor began to combine in my imagination and saddened me.

I began to feel at home in the homelessness of sadness, at one with dispossession.

Asthma gave palpable suffering to my privileged life (light bulbs, record players, balanced meals, blankets without holes, shoes with arch supports, electric trains, psychiatrists . . .). Why shouldn't Ivan Karamazov's absurd declaration that *there is no god because children suffer without reason* be applied to races, peoples, wandering tribes . . . ? I say absurd because even if there is a god I am certain he has nothing to do with suffering on this particular (earthly) level.

. . .

Rex and I were not close friends. Nobody was close to Rex, who, though in no way a grinder or a plodder, chose to spend his afternoons doing homework. He dressed like a gentleman without seeming too correct. He often wore a maroon-colored short-sleeved V-neck sweater with a zig-zag gray hieroglyphic sketch on the front. Rex and I would astound the class with our mathematical acrobatics, multiplying and dividing enormous numbers, continually erasing the blackboard to continue our lengthy calculations. Chalk sparked on the blackboard and flew around our heads. For some reason we were the only two kids who understood that the principles of mathematics were the same for large numbers as for small, that 4683×2772 is no harder than 6×7; it was just a matter of carrying out the board work and computing sums in our head. But this was work. This was not just talking. Mathematics was an introduction to limitlessness. Where mathematics was concerned, there was no limit.

. . .

I thought the mastery of long division was the key to the mystery. The recognition of infinity. There is no limit to what can be divided. We go on, being divided.

. . .

Even at the tender ageless age of nine, while I counted the time until *Love Me Tender* would appear in stellar black and white, I was painfully aware of how middle-class white people felt that white was right. I recognized, despite the pleasure I took from favoritism, the undisguised look of pleasure in the eyes of teachers like Mrs. Klein and (later) Miss Shapiro, because I was one of them, because in addition to whatever individual characteristics might have attracted them to me, they were profoundly relieved to be teaching a (sort of) clean-cut kid who (more or less) shared certain values, certain assumptions, who would not stand up on the chair when they left the room, unzip his fly, and treat the class to some butt wiggle and hand action with his penis; that I did not, even as I donned the camouflage of a tough kid, carry a switchblade or a roll of nickels to add punch to my punch . . .

·   ·   ·

Love Me Tender was about to open, and we surreptitiously circulated articles with stills. The girls mooned. James crooned. Karen L. lulled me with "Tammy." Paul was noncommital. Rex was beyond childish things.

Walking home, Ulysses and I recited the ditty that ran through the student body.

> Sap sucker
> Mother fucker
> Ass hole
> Blue balled bitch

I never tired of these lines and continued to repeat them silently when I was alone. It is not, I think, because of the crude rhyme or copious alliteration but because the last two lines disturb, distress, expectation. A word that was always run together, "asshole," is changed, estranged from itself, its familiar use, when it becomes two words, each of which demands, in this new context, equal emphasis, equal stress. And "blue balled bitch" was both shocking and confusing: I didn't know what "blue balls" were, but I knew that females didn't have balls—so what was the point? I was intoxicated by the senseless sound, the ambiguity of the transexual image. Did this abrupt, broken lyric, inherited from who knows where, purposefully transpose blue balls onto the bitch because she was a tease? Was she a bitch because she let the male motherfuckers go away with blue balls?

I began to divorce the sounds of words from their meaning. I was shocked that Sidney lost control when, in response to his "What did you learn in school today," I blurted out, "You are an asinine asshole" and burst out laughing. Yanking off his belt in fast forward, he not only spanked me more ferociously than he ever had but hit me all over, with his outsize, uncalloused hands, scratching my cheeks with his gleaming manicured fingernails, shouting, "*I'm* an asinine asshole. *I'm* an asinine asshole. If you ever call me that again, I'm going to give it to you with the buckle." Deaf to my plea that I was joking, he only gave up, having grown winded. I crawled under the coffee table and curled up in the "child pose," knees to chest with my hands over my head. The adult world had done it again: he was free to call me "schmuck," to say "take out the garbage, garbage," because we had a tacit understanding that he was playing, but my rare foray into what I thought was his mode of abusive teasing was greeted with straight rage.

.   .   .

I remember, my last semester at Kenwood, inwardly lamenting that Rex and I hadn't become better friends. We were walking in front of some shabby storefronts when Rex told me his father was a lawyer and that he was going to be a lawyer. Rex was doing all he could to live up to his father's image, but without *ressentiment* or evident strain. And Rex as a lawyer? I, who thought I could have talked my way out of anything, who could reduce our bully principal to tears while he shook me down about a ball I had not thrown through the window; I, who couldn't imagine anyone getting the better of me when it came to serious arguing or debating, sensed I had met my match in Rex. His motivation seemed higher, less personal. I reasoned that his investment in pursuing what he took for the truth may have had its roots in racial pride; it still wasn't quite as personal, as fanatical, as mine. I never saw either James or Ulysses—though I could see them squinting curiously at Rex from time to time—ever pick a fight with him.

Rex was good at being good. He was no prude, did not sit in judgment, but had no talent for mischief. I did not, when walking with Rex, grab a handful of coins from the nun's cigar box. I sensed that Rex was incorruptible.

4

Every month my mother would drag me to the Art Institute and try to explain cubism to me. I would already be starving (and still am when I enter a museum of any kind). We'd fight about what to do first: eat or look at art. When her will prevailed, we'd find ourselves in front of Cézanne's apples and while she yammered planes and illusion my hand reached out to touch—

¿DO YOU LIKE THESE APPLES

WHY ARE THEY YOURS TO LOOK AT?

¡WE EVICT THOSE WHO TOUCH THEM!

Doing the best she could to control her exasperation with my cloddishness, she'd point out Walt Kuhn's clowns, Ben Shahn's workers, Chagall's aeralists, Kandinsky's kaleidescopes of colliding worlds, Dali's time-burgers. I hated all the art children were supposed to like. I liked paintings without people, like Cézanne's Bay of Marseilles (which is housed there), where the paint has been laid on with a palette knife, where the water is as hard as the rocks and roofs around it; I could see just how intently he worked to be nature (not to imitate it), to get it down as it is on the canvas, its gravity—to not relax into fantasy, adding a lethal "personal touch" to what the objects were returning to the light—the discipline of going at it again to render the thing-ness and the density of the world, not an idea about the world.

My mind contracted and rebelled.

My mother was too knowledgeable about art for my own good. She had studied life drawing at the Art Students League in New York with Sam "Zero" Mostel and had given herself a private yet rigorous education in art history. Mostel thought highly of her work and of her. Once, she said, he begged her for a date by throwing down his hat on Fifty-seventh Street and dancing around it until she said yes—which she did not. She would let him walk her home but only if he walked a good fifty feet behind—a preview of her later divorce agreement, which decreed during the "custody case" that when my father had visitation rights to see me alone in Manhattan on Sunday afternoons my mother would follow at a distance of fifty feet. (She proved a good gumshoe: I never detected her watching us.)

5

The Ulysses who came to my birthday party was not Ulysses of the playground. This was a shy, charming boy who would never think of upsetting the lovely girls seated cross-legged in a circle in the living room. He seemed pleased that we were still best friends in spite of all that had happened between us. "This is cool, man," Ulysses confided to me in the kitchen. "Those girls, and all this food. Your mom's a good cook, man." This was heartbreaking. Ulysses sat outside the circle.

. . .

I don't remember ever going through a stage beyond the age of seven when, like most of the boys I see around me now, I didn't want to play with girls. I'm not sure why I never scorned the company of women, with whom I felt at ease even in the act of desiring them.

It was mutual: I was and was not a boy's boy.

. . .

Karen, Karen, and Karen. They all had the same loose-limbed, easeful gait, the same red-cheeked wakefulness and unself-conscious way of moving, and faces that would never tense with regret for what they were not—their reddish-blond hair darkening perceptibly below the topmost strands (pulled back tight and bound by a ribbon only); springy hair with a slight, yet lively curl that abolished any threat of perfection and made all of them approachable.

. . .

Prairie broke through concrete where I walked with Karen, Karen, or Karen, kicking the charred stones in Chicago's blaze of light, the knife-wind off Lake Michigan, the transient light in which I rubbed my body, steeped my skin, the light that witnessed the unbolted monster of pure space fling itself further and further upward: savage bits of disappearing white whirling about the water towers . . .

.   .   .

Tall, graceful, willowy, a strawberry blond and a Jew, Karen L. moved with an elegance and an assurance that was the opposite of my own frenzied awkwardness. I feared I would disappoint her, that I could never be smart or good enough for her, that she made a mistake in liking me, in not seeing me as worthless, subhuman, an insect. The fact that she was happy in my presence made me want to turn around when she was looking at me to see who she was looking at, who was at my back.

I preferred to pursue Louisa, the one girl who remained oblivious to Ulysses' secret charms—and mine, the one girl who scorned me actively, the only one who looked remotely like my mother. Dark hair, brown eyes, olive skin. She often wore fluffy white turtleneck sweaters, which heightened the beautiful severity and austerity of her features and her black hair. She was defined where the rest of us were undefined. She had made an effort to harden her sensual mouth. But nothing about Louisa was overdone. She was hard-edged, fierce, intense, and focused. I admired her quick absorption of matters which I could barely summon the will to attempt at all.

Louisa sat in the seat behind me in Mrs. Sheehey's class. Several times an hour I turned around to look at her, to engage her attention, mainly with pestiferous requests to borrow her eraser, but these efforts were usually met by a barely concealed sigh-groan and a scowl. Her resistance fueled, inflamed my daydreams. I thought it took courage for her to be as severe as she was. I respected her judgment: she saw through me, to me, to who I really was; she identified a menace.

My ruse for asking her questions during tests always failed. When I asked to borrow her eraser, she handed it over while keeping her head down, continuing to write with her free hand. I loved to watch her doing in-class assignments. I thrilled to the rigor of her logic, her clarity, both physical and spiritual.

When I saw myself through her eyes, I was filled with self-loathing; I longed to throw myself at her feet and pour my heart out with declarations of love and declamations about the "real" me, which would emerge if she returned my gaze; I longed to show her that I was at heart a deeply serious person somehow at odds with my situation.

Did she know I was an only child, that I needed attention so desperately because I was so lonely, lonelier than I would ever admit, that in spite of my sturdy appearance I was so depleted by asthma attacks at night that I arrived at school drained, a shell of myself, yet determined not to let on and give the teacher an excuse to keep me in at recess when dead leaves littered the ground or the air was too raw for my lungs or thick with pollen?

Couldn't she see I bothered her and played the buffoon only to get her attention? As all starved, diseased souls know: any attention is better than none, than being ignored, rendered nonexistent. I usually got the attention I sought, especially from girls and adults—though the very promiscuity of this charm propelled me later toward solitude. (An itinerant rabbi and his "family" are guests of a special sort: they are the center of attention, made to feel puffed up and important while their hosts are dutifully receiving them; but I knew, since I wasn't really part of their community [as well as only impersonating a rabbi's "son"], they would erase me as soon as I walked out the door.)

I wanted to tell her that I read books, even if they weren't the ones we were assigned in school. She would love the ingenious Zane Grey in which a sheriff, who can't let on that he's been temporarily blinded, insists on meeting a gunfighter in the street at noon, when the sun is high, so he can catch its reflection in a hand mirror and blind him long enough to shoot at the dusty shuffling of his boots, the clink of his spurs. *If she came home with me sometime after school, I would show her.* I fantasized her watching me hit clutch doubles, driving in three runs with the bases loaded for our class's nonexistent team to emerge victorious at recess, pass for touchdowns and make key interceptions, and of course being nursed back to health by her after being injured by all these heroics. This was surely wishful thinking even if I had been a better than middling athlete, because Louisa was utterly indifferent to such classic male behavior. Not that I could say what it was she wanted. Other than to be left alone by the likes of me.

. . .

If Mrs. Klein loved me too much in third grade, Mrs. Sheehey more than made up for it in fourth. Rigid, authoritarian, Mrs. Sheehey bossed me around with the phrase "right away quick" that sent me into overdrive, a dervish, ready for action with nowhere to whirl. It was her vocation to mark my every twitch. I couldn't relax in her presence. Every time I scratched my ear, she started. Every time Louisa heaved an exasperated sigh, Mrs. Sheehey's eyebeams attacked me. She was never off my case. Once I managed four days in a row without offending her, but moments after she threatened me with a gold star "to take home to your parents" for good behavior that week, I could not resist hitting Ulysses with a touch-down pass in the hallway on the way to the schoolyard before recess had officially begun . . .

. . .

Karen G. sat in front of me, and she was always happy to be pestered. When I gently tugged her braid like a bell pull, she screwed up her face in mock annoyance and handed me the compass, eraser, or "questions to be answered" I had not heard. She wore light cotton, light-colored dresses, crawling with small flowers, with a cast of round ivory buttons up the front. I wanted her to be my sister because then we could play together all the time; I loved the careless, absentminded way she'd curl up, cross-legged, on my bed and do her homework; I was touched that she could lose herself in my presence. She must have known I could see the white cotton flag of her panties in the splayed position she adopted, but she made no fetish of modesty. I didn't need to stare because all was offered— we were too intimate to "play doctor." I was in awe of her prairie beauty. But her after-school visits had a dark side, afflicted with a gnawing anxiety, that *she would leave*, get up and go as the clock neared five in the afternoon, stealing the brief serenity which suffused the room. I would no longer feel calm and whole: complete.

In the madness of my magical thinking that pouring out my heart to my mother would somehow enhance, make more real, the intimacy I shared with Karen, I had not armored myself in defense of her answer. My mother was happier at this time than she would ever be again: her being well used working for Dell Girlie contributed a lot to her high spirits. Sometimes my mother was my best friend. One afternoon when I had no one to play with and longed to try out my spanking new baseball uniform, I asked her if she would come out to the windy vacant lot across the street from civilization and pitch to me. She wore a loose cotton shift and a light-wool gray cardigan, which she loosely draped over her shoulders. It wasn't just that her slow underhand pitches were good but that I was inspired to play better when she was looking at me, that she was forced to spend most of the hour hunting the prairie for the lost ball. And since we played together and sang songs like Jimmie Rodgers's "Honeycomb" and "Kisses Sweeter than Wine" in the free-floating hours before dinner—choreographed so that she made the final preparations while I set the table—it felt right to tell her how swell I thought Karen was. Here memory stops short of event and invention, but I might have broached the subject of our future plans, as if by commiserating with the person dearest to me in all the world I could enhance, make more real, the intimacy I shared with Karen, and at the very least ensure further play dates in the future.

My usually playful, warm, empathetic mother vexed me with her dour, halfhearted response to the wild, beautiful creature I had just escorted home. No, *she* wouldn't "call her beautiful, Eva Marie Saint [whom Karen resembled] was beautiful. But then that little shift she had on wasn't very complimentary."

"You're beautiful too, Mom," I chimed in.

"A lot of people think so. When I walked down the aisle on my father's arm at a premiere, everyone thought I was Hedy Lamarr."

"You're prettier than that." I had never seen a picture of Hedy Lamarr, but her name implied a monolithic look, a unidimensional shell: black mane, white skin.

"Oh, I don't think so. Hedy Lamarr is gorgeous. But she's no actress, and that's why you don't see her in movies anymore; she can't act."

"I can."

"No you can't."

"I can. I made up a puppet show to put on tonight."

"You were so cute when you were little. Your hair was white. A director had his eye on you once when we were staying with Pop in a house he'd rented on Rodeo Drive in Beverly Hills. He asked me if you could take direction. 'Absolutely not,' I said."

There could be no more beautiful street in the world than a street named "Rodeo Drive," even if everything I knew about it I owed to snapshots.

"And?"

"That was the end of it."

"Maybe I could have taken direction from him. I could have tried."

I was beginning to have that hollow, nobody's home feeling.

"No. You couldn't have. And I wasn't about to humiliate . . ."

There's a phrase about gambling that Sidney liked to use: throwing good money after bad. The same holds true for our emotions. And some of us feel compelled, when things are going much worse than we expected, to continue hunting for the response we are after. Life is cruel and tricky here. As certain interactions approach disaster, catastrophe, or at least a collision that will definitely injure both parties (even if only one feels mistreated at the time), our fear is not, as is commonly thought, of losing the other's love. If someone manages in this way to infuse us with a negative feeling about ourselves, magnifying the feelings of emptiness and worthlessness we are struggling to relieve, grow through, and overcome, we fear that we won't be able to love them as wholeheartedly as we had before; something is irrevocably changed: it is not that we will be denied love but that we will be unable to love as we had wished, when it is precisely this ardency, this passion, this rage to love, that keeps us whole and hopeful. We are embarrassed by the people who hurt us so unnecessarily, who must assert their superiority at all times at all costs, out of their own bone-deep jealousies they would rather die than redress. And who among us has not caused pain to others in this way? Who is not, at times, sickened by the juggernaut of our own steamrolling cruelty?

My body registered my mother's put-down of Karen and then of me. Was it that I could not resist seeing how far she would go that I allowed myself one more chance, double or nothing, for her to respond in the way I wanted her to and say that she thought Karen was as lovely as I knew her to be?

"But, Mom"—would she hear the strain and anger in my voice and behind my question, she who, as I saw it, held the key to release me from this wave of unease—"don't you think Karen has beautiful hair?"

I reached out to catch the spike of contempt.

"Oh well," she paused and sighed, thoughtful yet casual: clearly this (leading!) question merited a considered answer. "I thought it was kind of mousy-looking, somewhere between, I'd guess you'd say, brown and blond, don't you think? . . . more like what you'd call . . . a dishwater blond."

Now that her criticism was no longer directed at me, my stuttering paralysis transformed itself into an empowering anger.

"No, Mom, she's beautiful; you just don't like her because she isn't fancy."

"That's not true. I didn't say I didn't like the girl. I thought she was very nice, very well behaved, unlike some of the children you bring in here like that . . . Eugenies . . . What does her father do?"

I stormed to my room and barred the door with desks, chairs, books, pillows, soldiers, and wept and let it be known I would not come out for dinner. And when Sidney came home and the threats began of what would happen if I didn't open the door, I opened the window instead, clambered down the fire escape, and ran. I ran as fast as I could for as long as I could. People were still coming home from work, bent low against the wind, their free hands occupied in keeping their hats on their heads. There were microphones attached to the dead leaves as they scraped the ground. The harsh November weather and the sinister leer of the streets where wild prairie and blunt high-rises took turns announcing their presence were nothing compared to the imaginary fears that wracked my waking and sleeping hours when my body was still. I was inflamed, on fire, on a tear, and with that much adrenalin pumping, any muggers, kidnappers, or child molesters would be wise to be afraid of me. High bales of wire under the floodlights against the fence offered another kind of shelter. And when I entered the gates of a military installation and conned the kind M.P. into letting me warm up in his booth for as long as I liked, I knew I had won and that Sidney would have to search for a long time before he discovered that his charge was not only not lost but well-employed, helping this lonely soldier check out the credentials of the entering cars. I was right, and when he stopped to see if the M.P. had seen "a little boy," I stood behind the soldier and said, "I'll only come out if you promise not to hit me, now or later." Strange how easy it was to get adults over a barrel if you were rough enough with them and held your ground.

6

Ulysses' life was unmoored. I envied him his freedom. If he could be *out at any hour of the day or night, so could I.*

His life was without constraints—without bourgeois bullshit, like the "family" being together at mealtime. Not that I had anything against the family, but sometimes I might have wanted to be doing something else when they were sitting down to a civilized dinner with candles. And the requisite regurgitation of the day's events.

.　.　.

One late afternoon Ulysses and I stopped at a coffee shop. "I'm thirsty," I said. "C'mon, man, I ain't got no money but a few pennies." I went up to the counter and told the waitress I had spent my allowance and asked . for a glass of water. The waitress delivered it—with ice and a napkin. "Can I have some water, ma'am?" The waitress put a glass of ice water and a napkin in front of Ulysses. He grinned. We sat and chatted, going round and round on the stools, until dark.
"Let's be blood brothers."

Ulysses pulled out his switchblade calmly and, with surgical delicacy, pricked my thumb.

.　.　.

Ulysses looked happy at my birthday party, but he knew that middle-class pleasures were not to be his. But this, a free glass of water, was an experience that could be repeated: it could exist outside social Darwinism and the "dog eat dog" lingo with which my father defined social life, along with, paradoxically, an almost mystical belief in Keynesian "laissez-faire" economics. One vicious fact about class structure is that the problem exists in an inverse ratio. The difference between our form of middle-classness and my friend's poverty was somehow an infinitely greater chasm to be crossed than that which lay between ourselves and the rich. The tragedy of economic difference resides in the calculus of this.

I see her now, the angelic waitress—dyed red hair, pallid green uniform— setting out the two tumblers of crystal before us, the transparence of the world. A glass of water: endless.

On Place: City and Country

I

*M*aybe there is no such thing as place, only experience within it, toward it, only our limited language that identifies cactus and kelp, mesquite and starfish, juniper and fir, and misses something else. Yet how to say what is on the other side of language? Impalpable relations, but how do you say that? What lies between things? That's too precise and imprecise. It's what you can't name about these things that is most important, the presence of the absence that is all around—which we forget in the thrall of human scale.

.   .   .

In *Pierrot le Fou*, Jean Luc Godard comes to terms with this gap by having Pierrot read a text on Velázquez while the camera details an agonizingly beautiful twilight (red and green pulsations) flickering on the Seine. We hear Jean Paul Belmondo's overvoice soothingly narrate in French as we read:

> The world he lived in was sad. A degenerate king, inbred infantas, idiots, dwarfs, cripples, deformed clowns clothed as princes. . . . Velázquez captured the mysterious interpenetration of shape and tone . . . a scattering of impalpable dust. . . . Velázquez is the painter of evening, of open spaces and silence, even when he painted in broad daylight, even with the din of battle in his ears.

The camera cuts to the actor who we now see reading to his less than rapt four-year-old daughter kneeling at the edge of the tub while he takes a bath.

.   .   .

There's a lot to be said for being back in New York were it not for the weather. Happiness in the country is a light rain in the fields, clouds brooding like disgruntled gods on the mountains; but here, waiting half an hour under a marquee on upper Broadway for a bus, it is misery incarnate, releasing the genie of squalor: the cut-rate open-air department stores (where the world is crowded into one room); the cut-rate unisex "beauty" salons where someone has taken care to cross out "$15" and replace it with "$11!" (as if this in itself were cause for rejoicing), the numerous black women with white children in their charge (as if it were the early 1950s, not the early 1990s) waiting, waiting (but what is time when you're getting paid for it no matter what you do?). Everyone's makeup runs in this humid closeness, everyone dissolves: can you reach your destination while the you that is you remains?

All that constitutes the unconstitutional self.

.   .   .

What a gift then to witness, in the city, the human element: the old man attempting to retain a little dignity in his gait as he struggles with three briefcases overflowing, an incongruous sight near the boat basin in the refulgent light this Labor Day weekend, and the lazy, playful demeanor of so many others, the band playing '60s rock in the batting cage.

.   .   .

Change, not place, is the inconstant constant. The same is true for being: it doesn't have an awning.

We reiterate what we lack.

The very fact that place is so often romanticized proves that it does not exist in the realm of real things. The spirit of places implies mediation by a sensibility, not the cats whom I witnessed tipping over D. H. Lawrence's urn. (Lucky phoenix whose ashes are scattered endlessly forever.)

If Laurie Anderson is right and "language is a virus," then "place is a language."

This is not to say I am not bound up in being where I am.

.   .   .

I found myself walking east on West Twelfth Street, when my eyes were drawn toward the left and an X ray of a pair of lungs, and I felt strangely embarrassed, more so than I would have been if I had looked into an examining room—how could they leave the blinds open when someone's lungs were on the screen?—and I was reminded of the scene in *The Magic Mountain* (which I read one summer in Colorado twenty years ago with a view of Pike's Peak to the right of my periphery) when Hans Castorp goes into shock at the sight (sign?) of an X ray and he recognizes the fact of his mortality through the insidious workings of disease for the first time.

Did I know the day was coming when, after holding off as long as possible, I would have to look at what the X ray divulged about my thoracic spine, in which the nerve roots, trapped within a realm of falling timbers, decay, and degeneration, let out their own cries for help for the dumb surrounding vertebrae, bone, and—somewhat divided—muscle? When nerves are unseated, roused from their comfortable beds, they are wont to strike out unrelentingly until the form of the skeletal architecture in which they are housed returns, somehow, to form.

.   .   .

Sweeping, torrential rains. The subways flooded. No way to keep warm in the apartment without crawling under the covers. The day is a continuum of events threatening to happen; the gauntlet of sawhorses and slickered police, the blinkered dray horses in the shelterless sky; the planes sulking on the runways, as if they'd been unfairly punished; the "A" lines in Far Rockaway, where my father's father carted sturgeon, shut down.

I never reached Far Rockaway: Riis Point was far enough. While Madelaine and Sam started to body surf, I set out walking in my swimmer's trunks, without sunscreen or so much as a dollar wedged between the nylon and my hip. I did not think ahead that several thousand other people, on what could easily be the last beach-Sunday of the year, should appear in the mere hour or so I would be gone. Under the unremitting blaze, I paced the wrong stretch of beach over and over in my search for where I had begun.

I interrogated every lifeguard, but the noon shift had come on. I admit to impatience. I think of us as carrion for time—and I'm always trying to escape.

. . .

The late September light climbing the balconies like fire; the heliotropic curling tendrils of the hanging plants; the propeller fans that barely stir the humid air; the electric angling of the walkers; the burlap shadow ransacking the khaki green trash can (how long can he breathe with his head down there?); the Gothic church whose elms and ivied walls I've walked below endlessly without learning its name; the white formica cafeteria of the college where they still sip rancid coffee and talk of eros, civilization, love's body. But in the lobby the philosopher's spirit hovers.

. . .

Cornelia Street. There's a copper-haired girl perched on a cement tub with her back to a tree, not leaning against the trunk but letting its shadow rest on her shoulder. I sidle down the street and try not to become overwhelmed with nostalgia when I smell the bread in Zito's bakery, or see the skinned rabbits hanging in the window of the butcher shop on Bleecker— this is where I spent my youth, a decade of wandering and wondering among buildings built to human scale.

In the late afternoons I used to duck into my neighbor the horticultural- ist's hothouse for some talk about cuttings and human matters. Once this young Englishman broke from his reveries about plants to ask, "Why does everyone in New York look the other way when you talk to them? Is it ambition? What's the hurry, I always say. What kind of juice or tea would you like? I've got—"

As people turn off West Fourth Street or Bleecker onto Cornelia, they slow down; they know it is a turn into the twilight, the brimming haze of suggestion; the afternoon is winding down. The light is climbing rapidly up the fire escapes—giving the illusion of mass through tenacity—and the abbreviated song of one wren will end not on the roof but in the sky. Someone kicks a pebble down the length of the street, and you can hear every tremolo of the roll, the subdued clack.

I always tell friends from out of town to meet me here, but they can rarely find the street—long and lovely in the lattice of shadows in the late afternoon.

.   .   .

St. John the Divine. A sleek maroon vehicle cuts across my path as I step off the curb, featureless faces behind the darkened window; I know I have entered another neighborhood. Sunlight on the cathedral's meticulous scaffolding—not sunlight but the late fall light, which adheres, gentle yet tenacious, to the cathedral vault.

Families file past, bartering with children, "You say bath and I say *Inspector Gadget* then bath." Water issues from the fountain in slow jets measured to the pace of the walkers and the sanguine, slow changing of the light. A disabled turquoise Checker cab catches the drift of the fountain's spray. Two men haul a goldenrod sofa, which is lost in the fading yellow of the decaying leaves and in light the color of the leaves.

It's late in the day, in the year, in the century; late in nature, flourishing life. Every second there's less and less. There's no longer a border separating the mad, the doomed, the hopeless.

City—even to say the word is somehow a violation—but of what? Not those who inhabit it but some naked gestus of the place itself, some preterite, preliterate, preternatural invention, some ur-place, a language of images.

.   .   .

Wanted: new strategies for dealing with life, with life's demands, as the cards are dealt. All card houses fall.

The stillness of the tree through the fissures of the windows—lending an ear. The autumn light falling, fading, on D's auburn hair.

I'm not thinking about it in terms of the calendar but of the radical change of weather from week to week, from oppressive sultriness to thunderstorms to the cold and brilliant clarity that afflicts us now. And the gargantuan stock-still half-moon resplendent in the night city sky. I have never gone to an astrologer, but the sheer existential fact of the light, the presence of the empyrean, the impossibly luminous, transparent, endless, hard, carved skies (folded, enfolded, layer upon layer), distances I feel myself falling into, compel me toward another mood as I anticipate the short, dark, cold days of winter (I remember, or know preternaturally?) which will soon—too soon?—quench these fires, these lusts. If you think me too romantic, I offer that I gather fuel for these observations from other people: what they say and what they do. And what they don't do.

These other people happen to be mainly women, which is not accidental either: there is less dissimulation about life and death with women than with men.

And I left out—children. When I came home this afternoon, Sam—with whom I had been swimming no more than an eternal hour ago—was rehearsing for Halloween and was genuinely scarifying as a vampire, having unearthed cape and teeth from his deep and spacious closet.

And Halloween, corny as it may sound, is usually a cold, dark, windy night—which is the earth's way of saying: pay attention to me, my magic is change; I lingered all summer, trotted in September, cantered through the azure of mid-October, then galloped off to darkness, impenetrable night.

I would grow tense in mid-October, in part because too many people pass through town. People are migratory creatures who modify their behavior through force of reason and "make their peace" with where they are and who they are—before the gates and jail doors of winter close.

Nothing consoles me more than to know that others have passed this way before. John Keats, whose lungs were soon to become more holes than lungs, noticed how on St. Agnes Eve the onset of the dark and cold crimped the style of rabbit and owl.

Life would be less painful—and less real—if these sensations of crystal skies about to shatter were less acute. Less grave, graven; carved.

. . .

It's taken five days since Halloween for there to be another day *qua* day. Another day that qualifies in the register of days. Subjectively. The others were—endured. In pain and with disbelief. When did my body become this frail vessel? Why did A, when I said the body is a frail vessel for the spirit, say she didn't think it was, that we couldn't separate the two, body, spirit (and the third—the mysterious third). I didn't mean to say *separate* but that the cruelty in the gap between our infinite longings and our finite groveling at the gates of what can be done, was at some times keener, more acute than at other times. Crueler.

Like the immigrant, tied to earth by his suitcase, without which he might soar over the rooftops.

A painter I know did a series of striped paintings in which a headless man in striped pants could be seen carrying a suitcase past the striped backs of chairs, up striped stairs: his verticals in dizzy contrast with the horizontal lines of the world. A man in motion. And her father, a traveling salesman, was always disappearing. We take our chances and make our chances. I like to think the headless man could oppose the inertial pull that underlies the mask of necessity, that he could have let go of his suitcase, whether it contained his own gear or "samples," and found new life, somehow, near. But what would he have done, hovering, beyond experience, in the aerial heights, when in need of love or water? What transitional object might assist the arc of his rising and falling?

. . .

The day is so perfect it disgusts me. I awoke not quite prepared—in spite of yesterday's unseasonal warmth—for the caressing sun. Mid-November's always been a bleak time for me and screamingly bleaker since my father chose the twelfth as the day on which to leave this world. So that last Tuesday night, though exhausted, I lay awake till dawn in vague nameless, wordless terror, images of him in this life edging toward ruin—and not.

I feel wretched walking around in this November heat. Give me snow. No, it's not the day, just exhaustion. My students resist and test me every inch of the way. I try to explain that in a poem sexuality can be dealt with obliquely; that if consciousness comes into being with a memory trace, they owe it to the reader to reveal some portion of their minds, of what excites them, rather than blunt statements of fascination and revulsion— "I'm hard," "I'm wet." One volunteered that she read Wallace Stevens. "What about eroticizing the weather?" "What?"

Hard to do today: a sullen drizzle. Weather of the groan and trudge. And difficult, difficult to swallow in late November when other expectations intervene. Difficult to resurrect a patterned variance out of the gray: More contrast is necessary. I leave the lights off. So is the light falling on the page *natural*? Particles interacting with particles. The result is—? Street cut in two. And so the question remains open?

Walking Broadway this morning in the uncharacteristic brightness I wondered how our thoughts and actions affected each other; I wondered if we read each other's thoughts unknowingly, as if our minds were pooled together and this caravan marching to the subway entrance were carrying out some inexorable law, and my returning to my room to put on Janos Starker playing Bach's unaccompanied cello suites were somehow necessary too, in terms of the collective . . . , or if—on this specklike earth—we carried on with choice and chaos.

. . .

Recognition of mortality as a precondition (precursor?) of ecstasy, of— and I *dare* to use the word—radiance—revelation. It's not mine; I don't own it. I can see it on others' faces as I walk the streets in the startling, mercurial, mid-spring light. Maybe these elations are only due us after long labor, I don't know.

.   .   .

A desert war brewed on the radio. I was driving north, toward the lovely suburbs, through an opaque mist that hung lightly over the Hudson like the one Kant says separates us from the things themselves, past the consoling place-names, Scars-dale, Larch-mont, White-Plains, New-Rochelle, when it came to me: Harrison is the place where my cousins the Wolfs live. I can't remember having met them even as a child, and they have children, close to my age, who would be my cousins, too. I pulled off the parkway to look for a mailbox marked WOLF. The fog didn't help. I couldn't make out any names. I was surrounded by the vast lawns. The crew-cut grass. The impeccable hedgerows. The distant, immense manor houses and empty tennis courts. Dwindling poplars. Drawn shades. Harrison is close to the river. I could live here; I'd walk along the banks and look at the black cliffs of the Palisades, not the smoke and signs of the factories that face the city. The suburbs are lonely. But it is lovely to drive through them.

I sometimes think of the Wolfs when I look at the diorama in the Museum of Natural History of the wolves running over the snowcrust at dusk, their tracks eternally planted behind them, their feet forever in the air, suspended. They are like the troops, shot in midair by the still camera, piling out of Blackhawk helicopters with blades thinned to a razor's edge in a sky scalded with oil smoke from the smudge pots of burning wells, runners hovering just above ground, about to take off over the desert sand.

.   .   .

I am getting ready to leave for Purchase, where I am teaching Wednesday afternoons at 1:30. I leave my apartment at 12:30 and go to the car parked across the street. I can't get the locks to open. I try them from every possible angle, then walk back across the street, where the building workers, wearing sandwich placards, are chatting among themselves under the scaffolding. I have such a terrible relationship with inanimate objects and technology that I'm still willing to entertain the chance that I am not doing something right—that my lack of expertise with keys and locks is the reason I can't get the door to open. I ask Willie, our even-tempered, considerate doorman, to help. He opens the trunk of his white Cadillac, parked right in front of the building, and withdraws a slender tube of lock antifreeze. First he tries the key every which way, as I did, then squirts some cold liquid into the lock. Tries the key again. No luck. "Someone jimmied your lock," he pronounces. It's now 12:45. It would take at least two hours to get from here to Purchase on the train (because you have to go to Grand Central, which is in the opposite direction, first, and then drive from the station to the school). I know I wouldn't be able to settle down for the rest of the day if I were not to go, and I hate the idea of making up the class another week, so I ask Willie if I can borrow his car. "Sure," he says. Then hesitates. "Except I want to keep my parking spot." "That's all right," I say, "I'll put it in the parking lot later." He flips me the keys and I'm off. I haven't driven a car with power steering in longer than I can remember. And the Caddy needs it.

· · ·

Driving home wildly, madly, in rush-hour traffic to pick Sam up in time from his after-school program at the 92nd Street Y—late because I had left the headlights on all afternoon and the battery had gone dead—I turned the music up to drown out the roar in my head. The ruin of everything around me seemed so real, the fact of that impermanance almost parodied, unscored by the names of the towns I'd passed. I used to mock commuters risking life and limb to get home ten minutes earlier to down a martini, and there I was, one of them, choosing to hug the wall rather than pull off and call and say I would be late and, once in Manhattan, tailgating taxis fearlessly, arrogantly even (I am not proud of this)—and when I got there, he was (understandably) sullen, cross—and when I told him how hard I'd driven to get him, he burst into tears. And then we had a quiet dinner, face to face, without a word, at the local Cuban Chinese restaurant where we go every Wednesday night.

· · ·

The unionized building workers strike and wear sandwich placards; they hover in doorways and under scaffolds and awnings day and night. Doing nothing's their real work. Construction crews spatula cement on the steps of brownstones, which will soon be "better than new." Drills in full gear. I couldn't hear a thought if I had one.

. . .

As the war intensifies I find it hard to think but am visited by a series of dreams, each of which takes place in a different place.

Dreams of Cities: (February 1991)

I

London fog in Manhattan.
A psychologist I overhear in the café
says, "children don't really understand
war, they're too literal." And while I stare
at the front page photograph of the collapsed
bridge in the Tigris, struck, split in two
by Allied Forces, the imprecise grayness
of its fall brings back photographs
of what might or might not have been
the monster of Loch Ness, that periscope
in mist. I put my eye

to that lens: sprawling green furrowed farmlands
fed by an immense lake, and this arable land
is worked by specks who on a closer look
are kids I went to school with in Chicago,
now convicts, whose prison, whose freedom
are these vast flat lands where a single body
escaping could be seen for miles even by

the naked eye—it doesn't seem like bad work,
turning the earth over with a shovel,
staring out at the calm lake's unbroken horizon,
just man and nature again though I can't see
where they go at night—what huts, what cells
await. I climb a grassy mound
and there, just beyond this pasture, I can see

Chicago, the sprawl of interlocking streets
and any detail I choose
plucked from the indefinite future, from possibility—
a newsboy on a bicycle
hurling a *Tribune* onto the stoop
in a quiet neighborhood of two story houses.

I want to go there—now—
there must be a train leaving,
from somewhere, any minute,
but the reformed juvenile delinquent
who now guards the others,
detains me on the platform—
after I have walked miles through marsh and pasture
to get there—loosening the burdock—
and asks where I think I'm going.

Chicago, I say, and try
to conceal my longing to get there.
That's where the others ran into trouble, he says.
Am I sure I want to go? Don't I want to stay here,
where it's green, and the air is clear,
and the corn is golden, have I looked
at it?—and he shows me some threads
of golden straw in his palms. No one
comes here, he says, no one
ruffles our feathers. What they've done
(you must remember some of them)
is forgotten.
But are they here for life?
(I just want to make sure.)

Maybe Chicago looks better than it is
from that distant hilltop, but I must
get there, soon, while the desire's keen,
and the smell of salt marshes
is not too far off.

2 *Oscillation: San Francisco*

My father, Charles, is half an hour late,
for an appointment on Market Street,

and in that time to kill I wander
through the mild fog where bodies float.
He'll make me late for my next appointment.
He might think I'm late.
It can't be easy for the dead to shave
and throw on a fresh polo shirt
and catch the trolley—but it isn't
easy for the living either.
And I can't remember who arrived first
to wait at the table in the gray café,
but once we're there, seated across
from each other, he's not happy,
rebarbative, even in death,
why, you mean you don't know why?

Do I think my malicious mischief
has gone unseen by the gods?
"Dad, I don't mind that you're late,
I don't mind wandering Market Street in the fog
but I have to meet a friend,
soon, in some state park's cafeteria,
and he doesn't like to wait.
I've known you all my life
but I've known him half
and I'm half-an-hour late."

In a restaurant high on a hill
my friend is finishing his meal.
He's part—yet not part—of another group.
He won't do more than nod a curt hello.
How much do I have to pay for half
an hour's lateness?
A sudden tremor jolts the earth,
rocking the table. The stone
foundations rumble. The strangers disperse.
A look of sheer panic crosses his face
as he stands and grips the red wood,
fixing his gaze on the rocks and fields
sprawled below the wide bay window.
Calm through the earthquake,
I look for a sign of feeling
and want to know why his face is set;

why he didn't do more than nod.
I wish he'd stop wasting our time on anger:
we know who kept me waiting,
and how, and where, and when, and why.

3

The train station converts into an airport.
They want me in Russia, the trip's free,
but that's not the part that compels me
now—the plane is small—the jet engines
too powerful for the body of an eight seater—
with a woman as pilot and no
co-pilot. What if you fall
asleep or have a stroke?
Then you fly it. Just watch what I do.
It's just raising and lowering, that's all
flying is.

4

The hilltop I am standing on is replaced
with Paris, a city as far
north as Alaska and still
under construction. Even in the cold
fog and dimness of February
there's action: wheel barrows, pickaxes,
boundary stones laboriously moved,
lovingly fitted and piled.
The hilltop's a turreted dome.
The separations between the stones—
gun emplacements.
The city sprawls inside these medieval ramparts.
No one's ruffled by what goes on
outside the wall, on the steep slope,
the sharp, abrupt rise
that makes transporting stones so hard.
I know that once inside the walls
of this ancient, homogenous world

I could let go of my tensions.
Paris, no matter how cold, sounded good,
but I wanted to be on my way,
suspended between destinations—
even if it meant being slung between
mule and carriage in a sack on a pole.

5

A nameless town half-a-dozen miles from Nice.
It's cloudy. The crowd's indoors.
I know my father would still want to go.
I'll fetch him from the lobby
of the multi-national-hotel-city-mall,
poured concrete made to look like a cave
and painted with the ancient hues of a ruin.
My stepmother intercepts me; she says
no roads lead to Nice, we'll have to stay
here all day, all week.
I didn't understand.
Who said anything about roads? Or cars?
My father and I set off,
carrying scarves knotted on sticks.
We never get to Nice, but I get far enough
to see (close up though we are miles away) a boy,
not yet in his teens,
pedaling furiously toward the sea
on a narrow, curving street,
taking the bumps of the cobblestones
easily. I didn't say
he reached the sea, the February sea—
a sludgy still mass, under a cloud-mat,
that laps at the pilings;
I had the distinct sense
that he was going to see someone:
a friend, or his grandmother,
who would take him into her stone
house and offer him some hot chocolate
and listen to the tale of his day—
an old peasant woman with whom he had a kind of pact.

He didn't need to reach the sea.
He lived within sight and sound
of it every day of his life.
The salt smell rises, even to this
mountain height and permeates the leaves
so you know what you're near though you can't see
the water through the trees.

6

A revised Mexico City.
Broad arcades. Striated facades.
The subtle sheen of moss in the entranceways.
Everyday discourse on the avenue
wide enough for the crowd to sprawl—
but everyone leans toward one entrance.
I turn left.
Only from this angle can you tell
the building has a fifth side,
with steps so narrow
adult feet would have to climb sideways.
I linger on the sidewalk, getting ready
to walk across the grass, to find a way
through this fifth side,
as if once I entered
I would never have to leave.

.   .   .

Unlike my fellow citizens who are glued to CNN annotating "ten thousand sorties" in less time than it took for the *Iliad* to unfold or for Achilles
to come out of his tent into the blaze to stand on the rampart by the ditch,
and rock the Trojan camp with his full-throated shout, I am listening to
the story of Ludwig, the drowned king, in German, on cable TV. Old
Europe with its terraced landscapes and reedy lakes tugs at my genes. I
recognize something, though I've never made it as far as Alsace-Lorraine.
I have the desire to regress, to release myself from the anxious instant
with its fragmentary, inessential yet necessary demands, to go where I
have not been, beyond "experience." It has something to do with fami-

lies, the acid dissolution of mine (what happens to the molecular structure of chemicals that are dissolved in acid?). My mother's in Florence, South Carolina, alone. My father jumped out a window because he felt an alien in Miami (lasting only three weeks). These are people whose lives were structured around intimate connections. (Is poetry a refiguring of community?)

. . .

There is still a straight and strict tendency to idealize nature, to see it as at least the potential realm of the sacred, and to see the city as the fallen world, utterly profane.

. . .

There are times when the avenues are so empty New York reminds me of an abandoned city in the desert. The sky yawns and stretches toward infinity through the sieve of streets. It's almost as if time were ticking—like a taxi meter. You can live a long time in one place and still be a stranger. No one knows anything about you beyond a sketch they could give the police if "something happened" ("often left his apartment around noon").

Yesterday at dusk, the facade of a dignified old brownstone was an unearthly pink—yet the sun itself, glowing in the cold over the purple water of the Hudson, was yellow (lemon? Dijon?) It lit up the burlap piled in barrels, the curlicues of wire on top of some scaffolding. Walking through the archway of the monument at 100th Street and Riverside Drive, into a wall of white light like the tip of an unseen flame, I thought I was in the desert, passing through a stucco section of Phoenix, cleaving to the shadows cast by trees put there for shade; I wanted witnesses! It's as if the city had returned to its elemental self. The wreckage, the ruin, was gone.

I long for those few moments in the day's cycle when borderlines dissolve, when continuity—the "illusion" that the next moment flows inexorably out of this one, that the actions we commit are in some way necessary, inevitable—is ruptured.

. . .

Have crossed the park twice already this morning. Buds on the dogwood. Rain falls with pleasure on my head. It's the first day on earth. The park is never more primeval than in the rain. No one will sell me an umbrella at this hour. Even the street vendors are still asleep. Sam's diminutive transparent plastic umbrella, with Mickey Mouse in various postures wielding various clubs, racquets, and bats, is sturdy. It's not big enough for both of us to stand under but it lasts.

I desire for the afternoon to last forever, now that it has begun to rain again. To play with Sam and his "men," his transformers. He sets some to his left, some to his right. "These are good guys, these are the bad guys . . ." But the one he can break in two and reassemble as a seamless truck is allowed to be both good and bad.

.   .   .

Bright Tuesday, the wrong morning for the sun to be so prodigal. Too much to do, run these errands within the circumference of this block, down West End to Broadway and 100th to the Xerox, then to the pharmacy on 99th, the Korean Market for milk—almost at 98th—then back to the Chinese laundry on 99th but cut back from Broadway (though I was sure I'd be a day early). I have to plan my route to meet M. at Citicorp a shade after one. Why Citicorp? Because he feels drained when he gets within range of the university at which we poets are privileged to teach. *But why Citicorp?* I don't know; normally I ask, normally I am obsessively fussy about plans. I once met another "M." there (I can't remember why we chose Citicorp or who had to "be around there"), and I was impressed by the selection of restaurants and the infrared glow that vanquished any questions I might have had about the mall's modernity. I once killed time there waiting to hear Zbigniew Herbert read at St. Peter's Church upstairs. I brought my class—so rare were this poet's visits to America—but he didn't show. I knew he wouldn't come, and if his health was so fragile, why did he accept the invitation in the first place? Getting to Citicorp even from here is a feat, unless you get off the subway at Columbus Circle and walk east, across town, in the sun that belongs to everyone.

.   .   .

As I cross a Broadway island I watch a cop prod some poor creature with a nightstick: he's rigged a blanket with a shopping cart filled with empties, and a cane between bench slats to serve as a kind of tent pole—an admirable impromptu shelter—and he looks properly indignant when the man-in-blue jostles him in his hovel. What struck me was not any sudden compassion but admiration for his transient domestic sense; it was the kind of hovel one might form slowly over time, in a tunnel, but not overnight. I had to move on—but I thought for an instant I could almost see shelves stocked with herbs and preserves, so self-sufficient did this shelter seem until the nightstick let in the light of day.

. . .

My bags weighted down with books and papers, I ride the IRT across from a black man who is still somewhere in his twenties, handsome, with dreadlocks that have matted and grayed—a well-worn dustmop. He displays the stump of his leg—amputated just below the knee—proudly and flexes it like a pilot testing a wingflap. His "coat" is the erstwhile lining of a coat—mattress stuffing. Now he's scouring every centimeter of his body, picking the lice from his sores and scars. He asks for nothing. And it takes another drifting homeless man to flick a dollar bill onto his lap and call out "brother."

. . .

I pass a single room occupancy hotel where outpatients and derelicts lived before there were so many homeless. There is a man suspended up there, tangled in ropes and hooks and pulleys, kicking his feet like a swimmer. Fresh white paint shines on the walls and his equipment; his overalls are white. His head and neck I cannot see, but I assume he had hoisted himself into the dark window for a reason—that he was there to repair something. Even headless he had something of the daredevil about him.

The moment of composition—the sky whitening at the edges yet otherwise blameless, unimpeachable, the nine-to-fivers shuffling toward the subway, the grocers stocking the bins, the streetsweepers, and everything seen through the filter of a sleepy eye, fuzzily; the jackhammers heard drowsily, muffled by the remains of sleep.

Waking is the day's disaster—full waking is where "composition" ends. Only subattention is useful. (As Sam demonstrates when he looks distractedly and with wobbly bat at a ball he will smash into the trees.)

A poem is the sum of subattentions, the transcription of a command.

.   .   .

Walking, the other night, up West Broadway toward Canal street, I was struck by how the city opened up at certain points and the architecture seemed to welcome its inhabitants, giving them space and a sense of immensity. Even the color of the brick, a less than blood red, seemed welcoming. I stopped on Canal to buy an apple. The fruit vendors had bunches of limp and wilted grapes and stacks of bananas, no apples. The cardboard on which the fruit lay looked bruised. When I asked why there were no apples, the vendor replied, "Chernobyl." I thought he was saying something in a language I did not understand and asked again. "Chernobyl."

I had to have an apple. A greengrocer appeared on the next corner, beside a hole in the wall selling rows of decapitated fish. I was overcome by the smell of mackerel. The red meat of the dead fish. It was glorious, the Eskimo icehouse in lower Manhattan. I picked an apple from an overloaded bin. And when I turned onto Walker Street, it was redolent with the smell of garbage strewn wildly, freely, everywhere—I added my apple core to the heap—as some beggar was entering the hole in the fence before a vacant lot where garbage, junk, and clothes were strewn as if burglars, searching for some one thing, had emptied all the drawers and cabinets onto the floor. . . . He entered the lot with a calm expression and slow, even, determined pace, as if it were a supermarket or a department store.

.   .   .

A late Sunday afternoon in May. Most of Sam's friends are away at their country houses.

We're in the clearing, a small island bordering Riverside Drive and Riverside Park. A muddy mini-baseball diamond. Bat relaxed over the little boy's shoulder, his hands and wrists relaxed; no empowering of stance and gesture but when the ball comes he moves, and swings, and all of him is behind it.

Every time he pulls the ball down the imaginary third-base line I get to walk toward the Drive and glance beyond the rusty fuzz on the green benches to the river where gulls preen, and a warm, whitish light in the damp air blends light and dark, surface and depth, the almost chestnut-colored particles and the hot yellow of forsythia.

The small, whitish, two-engine propeller plane flying low and quietly, its rounded engines and wings, the rings that keep the propeller in place, looking like it is made of something lighter than metal, like porcelain—delicate, tenuous, yet strong enough to withstand the pressure of the upper atmosphere.

I pitch a "soft" hard ball, underhand, slow, to the outside right corner of the "plate" ("draw a triangle, Dad") to encourage the kid to hit away from where cars pass without a break in stride and the atomized leaves and pine needles blaze on the greening parapet overlooking the Hudson.

. . .

On my last walk on Fifty-seventh Street before leaving for the hills of Vermont, I found nothing I wanted to look at but people. One young woman, with a single braid in her blonde-brown hair, and a black cotton dress, and intense eyes (worthy of many Italian Renaissance masters), and a muscular awareness and singularity of expression and relaxedness of frame as she carried her lunch back to her office (or do I assume too much?), made me think that everything conspired to make me notice her, the street itself, the domineering buildings.

2

Vermont. The strange widening expanse of mountains, a rugged but welcoming landscape, altogether verdant, *complete*, altogether mysterious, harsh and Edenic, if you subtract the contemporary influence of malls and outlets, homogenized America, where anywhere is everywhere and nowhere. There's a brook in back of the rented house where you can fish for trout; a wood-carved and clayey (and dissembling) statue of a bear beside a stagnant pond which flows over a small dam into the brook; a disused sugar shack (foully moused-up); a "barn" complete with hot tub, broken pinball machine, and buffalo head; plethora of family photographs; low ceilings (I will spend the summer bowing). Rocks are massed in delicate congregations: they *bulk* without overwhelming.

Towns keep a certain distance from each other, and so do people. And so do people's houses from each other in the towns. People have a sense of proximity but do not demand a closeness—only contact, fleeting but consistent.

The lakes and streams that spurt up off the main roads look like they should be further from such common access. Someone fishing in sight of the main road can be engrossed, lose himself, be transformed, without a more violent separation from the possibility of being seen by others.

(Is New York the only city where you might have striking and intimate conversations with someone in your building whose name you do not know, who appeared at your door (in your life?) one evening with a child in tow . . . ?)

There's a genial relationship with the land in Vermont. And yet there is no question of a surplus: life is hard; survival. Distance from the sea reduces fantasy. There's a radiance of farms, rolling hills, zigzagging fences, blue silos, that could not go unnoticed by those who work the land. That radiance and grace is the *real* payment for their labor (is the reality).

Radiance? Black ice, having to crawl across the road when it's twenty below. Winter: Dürer clarity of weeds on embankments; the wind, vociferous, at the door like a confluence, a conference of ghosts. One winter in Cabot I lay awake as the wind at the rim of the world whirled the snow around the window; Sam thumped to the warped wood floor again and again and again, unwieldy anchor, tying the house between the sheets. At least, by the fourth time, I was down there, waiting, to catch him.

.   .   .

The freeze is heightened by sun glare off the snow. Nothing to be done except keep the fire going.

So we went for a walk, we tested the mountain, Snow White was on the one channel, and Sam says, "I'm too big to be a dwarf, Mommy's Snow White—who can I be?—" says he's going to "sit on the roof till there are more and more stars" and then he's going to "put out the fire."

It's not life that is too short, I thought, only our lives.

. . .

I must add snow-blindness to the list of my deficits—will I have time to learn about myself what might in time be of some use to others?

. . .

No flesh on the roads, only bundled outline with eyes.

These are walls only the snow has put up over the windows, the true storm windows: the storm.

An icicle hangs like an ax handle from the telephone line. To some, ice is an invitation. The men persist in ice fishing with axes. They stand thickened in layers of clothing.

Stoking the woodstove, my wrist and Sam's forearm are seared. The sky swaps roads with the weather: black ice shows up what's under, what's above.

. . .

And when the temperature rises and the sky clouds over, it feels terribly cold and cold in a way that another layer of clothing wouldn't help—

. . .

Boat-shaped snowflakes, then drifts, mounds to speckle the earth's surface, then rain, the pouring of a stream through blockage of ice; ice that could interrupt the flow of time, as water runs like time through the timeless white.

The snow never falls straight down, never plummets; black ice never settles on the roads; it contracts, clenches, bears down. The blizzard is the origin of seeing and of silence.

That's not wind we hear in the upper atmosphere. The blizzard comes as we knew it would—in a blessed flurry of chaos. The snow I now see falling is rising, just as Madelaine, backing out of the driveway onto slick ice, creates an occasion of return.

. . .

The snow rose, swirling over each valley's horizon; it scours every cranny of the north.

Only by falling can we begin to rise. It's always a matter of walking to nowhere, of the feet knowing where and where not to go in the abysmal snow. Every instant the body announces: what may be is. Only when falling do we cease to feel our own weight. I need this principled magic now in my life. The carnivorous sky erases sight.

Repetition's another human gilding of the inanimate, another flux-arresting construct. The bobcat's tracks were gone this morning.

. . .

The omnivorous sky erases sight. The blizzard swallows hill and stream, has left only a croaking solitary crow to awaken the distance. Jouncing downhill in a sled, Sam holds his ears as the water squeaks and whistles through the stream's freeze. I don't know what led us north this winter, but we may find out.

✦

It's so difficult for me to learn my way, to remember which turns to take. This is high, burgeoning summer, time for a melt-down. It cheers me to see people letting loose, dressed down, more skin than fabric. The light imbues what it lands on, wraps, with a kind of aura, a noncolor in the after sky.

New England domesticity: the signs with their suggestion of comfort and insularity. Is this a deeper sanity, a kind of wisdom centuries deep, or an act of back turning, a rejection of the conditions of the present, fraughtness and danger and peril?

. . .

Sam and I go to swim in the pool at Stratton. Blankout haze, humidity. We make a deal: After we play I can swim laps for half an hour while he entertains himself in the water. We're unexpectedly joined by a new friend of his, a New York kid whom he met at camp. It may or may not be relevant that his friend, also six, is black.

I'm swimming, working out the stiffness in my neck and shoulders, when I feel someone's eyes on my back. I swivel around and squint through my myopic eyes and fogged goggles to see a man behind the glass door that leads into the pool from the lobby. He's portly, middle-aged, sporting a walrus mustache and wearing glasses, dressed unassumingly in cranberry polo shirt and tan khakis. He seems to be smiling. I shake off my unease and get back to swimming. But the unease will not lift. I look at the boys jumping and splashing. They're all right. Nothing wrong. But the unease will not lift. After another half a dozen laps I stand up to stretch and look around again. He's there, staring at me. A few more laps and I look again. His eyes move from the boys back to me. I would be exaggerating to say I felt a sense of menace: I just wanted him to remove his gaze. I'm tempted to tell him that his gaze is annoying me, and I decide to let it pass until he does it again. There was also the chance that this sheepish-appearing "accountant" is just killing time while his wife or companion works out. But then he's in the locker room when we go to shower, wiping his sweat-drenched forehead with paper towels.

Driving home, Sam says he's hungry.
"We'll be home soon."

"But I *can't wait!*"

"There are some pretzels in the back."

"I want some pretzels."

"OK, but I have to pull over to get them."

We pass several private driveways, and Sam urges me to go down one—any one. I explain why I'd rather not if I can find some public place.

"People might feel intruded on."

"What's—intruder?"

"Did you see that man at the pool today who was looking at us?"

I expect a desultory answer or a "*what* man?" but I've never been able to predict one of Sam's responses.

"Yeah. That creep. Why was he looking at me all the time? I wanted him to go away."

"I did too."

"Well why did he keep on looking at me?"

"Was he looking at Ricky too?"

"Yeah."

"He was looking at me too. And he was in the locker room when we went to take our showers."

"I didn't see him in there. Why did he keep looking at me?"

"I don't know, but we felt he was intruding on us even if there's no law against it. Next time, if you feel that way, tell me, OK?" Long sigh. Long silence.

"Yeah."

This is the night of the great summer storm. Lightning flashes in the yard, power goes out. Sam drags his blanket in to sleep on our bedroom floor. We light candles: it looks like we're about to hold a seance. I'm telling him a bedtime story. A sheriff has just entered the scene when Sam interrupts.

"A *fat* sheriff. Like that man at the pool. The invader. Why was he in the bathroom combing his hair?"

"I thought you didn't see him there."

"I did. I don't like that man. I'm afraid to go to sleep. I'm going to have bad dreams."

An hour's event, endless unraveling.

.   .   .

There is the moment when you pause, taking the curve in the road, and a river appears; and beyond it on the hill, in the haze, are the house, half in light and half in the shade of maples, layered and stacked, spread out on the hills over the river, in the hazy shade; and it lasts a moment only—that is how long the respite, the relief, lasts. No small thing! It is a garden and it is after the fall. The stream is a curving ripple ladled, not gouged, out of the earth. The sun rises, frees the landscape of encrusted life—not the whole past, just that which obstructs movement. Even the cobwebs seem airier. Roads fork steeply east and west. The roads fork clearly in the early morning light, forcing the walker to make a quick decision. Roads, forks, leavings, traceries, incline gulley ditch—sign—turn left—stop. The sun, invisible, lights up creaking boughs and poppies, lights a path through the woods, meandering streams.

When the moon gets caught behind the black maple trees and the blue that lingers at the edge of the sky late at night, it is faint, almost colorless. One mountain blocks out another, the ski trails are no longer used. A monarch butterfly takes so long to finish perusing one grass blade I could have walked twenty city blocks.

.   .   .

Driving, as into an infinite—what? Expanse. Expanse folded within expanse, curved within space. The unrelenting green, thick, impervious. The immense breasted hills that reared above the highway, dense with evergreens. You have to look hard before the green falls away anywhere here and your eye is granted the respite of a rocky path.

.   .   .

A family of beavers has taken over a pond at the end of our road. The big one doesn't react when we stop by, but his mate and little one are cautious, quite cautious, and circle and crisscross the pond, going under at strategic moments, while he goes on dining with the grace of an epicurean at his endive and arugula salad at the Four Seasons. But when they start thwacking their tails, we know that we've outstayed our welcome.

.   .   .

This old house has an inexhaustible repertory of noises. If it's ghosts, they're doing nothing special—slam window or door, creep up and down creaking stairs, switch furnace off and on, turn log over. They make noise with a rhythm that's consonant with daily life. I think someone's breaking in. Someone has broken in. These are the conditions.

. . .

Another noise, a door slamming hard, a garbage can falling down in the barn; it's someone, something, or the wind; and when I scan the four corners of the landscape quickly, I see a woodchuck rowing through the meadow. Maybe he is the source of the sound, but he still can't account for it; it's not night; he's not rummaging in the garbage cans. I'd vote for the screen door, but since it's always so pressed to the jamb when I go to open it, I'd better guess again.

The house is infested with crickets. I found one on the stairs last night, and this morning he still needed an assist out the door. (Who says insects are at home in nature? They suffer from infirmities too. The cricket might be injured. I might have to make him a splint.)

It is never silent here, not with this din of cicadas, with this roar of brook water. Goldenrod is an undercover agent for the weeds; the grill has stayed balanced precariously on the stone fence all summer, even when winds from the hurricane caused the trees to wave their arms frantically and hammer wetly on the windows to be let in.

. . .

Gray morning. Only the barn's tin roof is silent in the stillness. I have already missed the parade. The mountain my son's day camp is on—bought by foreign interests—is open. He stayed home yesterday, thinking he was sick because his mother was sick, so today he goes, though it seems strange to treat this Thursday the fourth as a normal day. We told our friends not to come because Madelaine's virus might still be contagious, and other friends could not come because one of their mothers was dying.

A holiday of cancellations. An epic of unevent—except to find the oval pond rimmed by willows and canoes.

I hope our forefathers won't be angry. Don't imagine that the dead are inert. It's no accident that when you're driving in the country the markers you notice are all graves. "Go past the cemetery on the left until you get to the big white barn."

. . .

Sam doesn't talk much about death, but during a tête-à-tête with him at McDonald's in mallish Manchester I say I know him pretty well, and I know he won't ever walk across a street, much less a highway, alone again even if the "cars stop for him"—as he keeps saying they did—until I tell him it's all right; and he says, his voice ragged with impatience, "Daddy, you don't know me *pretty* well, you know me *very* well." I shouldn't have left him alone in the car, but he was absorbed in fitting together the parts of a police car and getting the spectacularly androgynous driver to stay in his or her seat, and he never crosses the street alone in New York.

The country's dangerous.

What it is to be six and to half-know what you should and shouldn't do, for your own good, to stay alive? When I was his age and my new stepfather left me in the car while he ran some errands, I let go of the emergency brake on a steep suburban street and thought it was all over as the car steadily picked up speed, when I glimpsed a man in a hunter's cap frantically signaling—I remember his earflaps—and bits of strangers starting from the sidewalks while I ducked under the wheel and they pushed the car back up the hill.

. . .

In the video store in Londonderry: a not unhappy and quite alluring woman in turquoise nylon jogging shorts, with two children in tow, clothes like an afterthought, the cotton and the sheer. I did not look at her breasts as she leaned forward to get a drink of water in her sleeveless T-shirt.

The immense propulsion of lust, endlessly quizzical. The wild dramatically cut back, the thickets secretive, rife with longing—mimicked by the cries of grouse and quail—and the lovesick rustling sounds, like great committees meeting in trees. Nothing the body cannot wander into.

.   .   .

After days of wind and rain and hurricane mornings, this sudden burst of sunlight is a shock. The return is to clarity. The maple trees, the brooks, the cedar waxwings. Two women talked on the porch. I listened and watched the two becoming one in one shadow: mine.

.   .   .

Sam is not of two minds when he declines to chase a ball into a thicket where bees hum. His hatred of bugs is legendary. The sounds of the woods disturb him. He has not learned how not to fear all that crackling and rustling. It always sounds like there are microphones in that brush. I realize that he hears, as the wind blows through the trees, animals. "What happens if there's a raccoon?"

Refract: aphid, beetle in the peony, spider on my leg, daddy-long-legs, a small garden so slimy, so full of ooze and chaos it commands my gaze. I enter that thicket warily, hoping not to incite the black and gold, the lovely buzzers. After mosquitoes a bee seems benign, like a parrot you might carry on your shoulder.

.   .   .

And glory in many forms comes in the color of goldenrod: from Sam's mop of hair to his inside-out polo shirt and grounded soccer ball, to the bees fattening in the day lilies; as if yellow had petitioned heaven for a slight change of tint—like taxis in the rain on late fall afternoons—and the leaves darken as they call up the word. The world. Goldenrod—still wedded to August. Goldenrod: not the weed, the color.

·   ·   ·

Hamilton Falls. The torrent poured. The rock pools filled and emptied; change the only constant. Only the brave dived in.

Some said the ladder was fastened to the rock pool to help swimmers climb down; others said it was there to keep you from being swept away, hurled to the next level, in case you fell in.

Have you ever met a reliable witness?

A cemetery on the hill: the children's graves were lined up in a row, half-a-dozen "Cummings" born one year and dead the next.

·   ·   ·

I go out on the porch to be closer to the rain. I can't make out a single thread but hear the leaves loose their raindrops and the roof throw down pans of water on bushes that are already turning color in early August; and amidst this sound, penetrating, ubiquitous, through some mysterious arrangement between the mist and light and haze verging on azure, I can see, dimly, mountain unfold on mountain, hill on hill, curved within unrelenting green, primeval, brooding.

·   ·   ·

Walked out into a meadow late last night. A faint blue light rimmed the sky's edges. The trees were black, like nothing else around them, from the grass to the barn. A shooting star squirted past.

I turn back to the ultramundane clothespins, hammered into the ground to hold a string taut for Sam to play at marbles within.

That's a galaxy too. But more like the Milky Way is the lace bodice of a nightgown.

·   ·   ·

I invariably feel a surge of pleasure when, after crossing the bridge, I arrive at the junction of Route 100 and Middletown Road. I shift into neutral and pause, and take my longest breath of the day, deciding whether to turn left and return home through Londonderry or go straight and take the shortcut. Sam always encourages me to go straight ahead because that's "the back way," and since he was old enough to talk he's been a connoisseur of back ways.

.   .   .

Anything like hurry can only destroy the rhythm of the spaces left between the cultivated and the wild—dwellings, lawns, geometric fields, and meadows where weeds sprawl and grow tall—and offer open-ended invitations for you to let go of whatever you can't afford to lose. Or what it is you think that brought you here.

The back way is like a song on the tape deck I don't want to end, don't want to "rewind." It is perilous to hope too hard for what comes without hope and when the will is quiet.

.   .   .

I am trying (always) to get at something, through "the back way." How else to put forth those conditions except by analogy?

One major error in thinking in our time is in imagining that knowledge is rapidly progressing, that one form of knowledge "replaces" another just so.

Adventure is not something one seeks but an attitude toward experience. It is this possibility which psychologizing has in part destroyed. If living is not an adventure, it is nothing. For me, surviving is its own adventure—and there are many nights when, no matter how cozy my immediate surroundings, I feel as if I were hunkered into the base of a cliff for shelter. Is there ever poetry without a sense of discovery? The chance factor is part of every step. (That coyote might throw you a glance from which you might never recover.)

And so Blaise Cendrars set off on the Trans-Siberian Express, and Emily Dickinson, having done her chores, retired to render her further permutations of the Pascalian notion that all human unhappiness stems from our inability to stay quietly in a room.

Poetry rebels against notions; its essence undermines the norm of notions, the gloss, the glaze over life; it opposes everything in daily life that conspires against these profounder energies—conspires to level.

But modern life has made people think that life is everywhere except here— for even common living can be a form of flight.

.   .   .

Coming back to Vermont after a week in the heat of Florence, South Carolina, where I have been tending to my stepfather's last days, the sky seems an insult, a reminder of a beauty that is too fleeting for the mind to grasp, a beauty that, like death, is somehow unspeakable. I've never been one for flowers (I prefer butterflies), but now I see the reason we love them blooming and dying under our gaze. Even the sky with its pearly clouds, even the grass, seems unjust. A luxury only the living can know. And living is just that, each instant, though habit numbs us to this fact.

On the bus, moments of relief in the rain, then the windows darken again, and I think just how much life is like mourning, how emotions and feelings succeed one another moment to moment in a way that saves us from complete despair. It's not known how much of mourning is for ourselves or for others, but we mustn't cleverly underestimate the latter. Others come to dwell in us. They become part of our cells, within our cell.

ABOUT THE AUTHOR

Mark Rudman is Adjunct Professor in the writing programs at Columbia University and New York University, editor of the literary journal *Pequod*, and recipient of numerous awards. Among his other books are *Diverse Voices* (1993), *The Nowhere Steps* (1990), and *By Contraries* (1987). His most recent book, *Rider*, was published by Wesleyan University Press in 1994.

UNIVERSITY PRESS OF NEW ENGLAND publishes books under its own imprint and is the publisher for Brandeis University Press, Brown University Press, Dartmouth College, Middlebury College Press, University of New Hampshire, University of Rhode Island, Tufts University, University of Vermont, Wesleyan University Press, and Salzburg Seminar.

LIBRARY OF CONGRESS CATALOGING-IN-PUBLICATION DATA
Rudman, Mark.
    Realm of Unknowing: meditations on art, suicide, and other transformations / Mark Rudman.
        p.   cm.
    ISBN 0-8195-2220-1 (cl). — ISBN 0-8195-1224-9 (pa)
    I. Title.
PS3568.U329R4   1995
814'.54—dc20   94-39701
∞